A note on BLACKWATER

Michael McDowell has taken on a
remarkable challenge with a novel the scope
of BLACKWATER.

His work has ranged from the contemporary
novel of horror set in the American South
(THE AMULET, COLD MOON OVER
BABYLON, and THE ELEMENTALS) to the
extravagantly detailed novel of America in
another time (GILDED NEEDLES and
KATIE).

His fullest powers are mustered now in his
six-part novel, BLACKWATER which Peter
Straub, author of GHOST STORY says "looks
like Michael McDowell's best yet...it seduces
and intrigues...makes us impatient for the
next volume." Straub says McDowell is
"beyond any trace of doubt, one of the
absolutely best writers of horror;" Stephen
King calls McDowell "the finest writer of
paperback originals in America;" and the
Washington Post promises "Cliffhangers
guaranteed."

MICHAEL McDOWELL'S
BLACKWATER: II

THE LEVEE

AVON
PUBLISHERS OF BARD, CAMELOT, DISCUS AND FLARE BOOKS

BLACKWATER: II THE LEVEE is an original publication of Avon Books. This work has never before appeared in book form.

AVON BOOKS
A division of
The Hearst Corporation
959 Eighth Avenue
New York, New York 10019

First Avon Printing, February, 1983

AVON TRADEMARK REG, U. S. PAT. OFF. AND IN OTHER COUNTRIES, MARCA REGISTRADA, HECHO EN U. S. A.

Printed in the U. S. A.

WFH 10 9 8 7 6 5 4 3 2 1

In THE FLOOD, Volume I of the BLACKWATER saga, Elinor Dammert is discovered awaiting rescue in a curiously undamaged room on the second story of the nearly destroyed Hotel Osceola in Perdido. The only person still remaining in the flooded town, she tells her rescuer, Oscar Caskey, that she had slept through the hotel evacuation four days earlier and has been trapped, without food or drink, ever since. This will not be the last of the strange events involving Elinor and water—some of them horrible, some merely inexplicable—that the town will witness.

Elinor soon charms James Caskey, Oscar's uncle; wins the undying affection of little Grace, James's daughter; and incurs the enmity of Mary-Love, Oscar's mother. Mary-Love watches with increasing rage as Elinor insinuates herself into the bosom of the Caskey family, snaring the heart of Oscar and marrying him behind Mary-Love's back. But Mary-Love has her revenge. If she can't have Oscar to herself, then neither can Elinor—for with the continually unfulfilled promise of a house as a wedding gift, Mary-Love keeps the newlyweds under her own roof, biding her time.

Only when Elinor gives birth to a daughter do she and Oscar make their escape. However, to gain their own home they must relinquish their baby daughter to Mary-Love. She will accept nothing else as replacement for her son; Elinor is willing to pay the price.

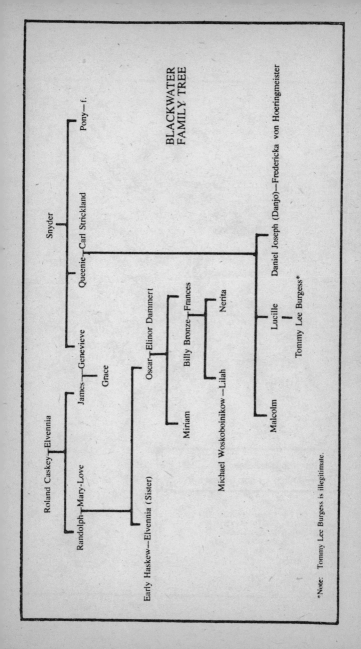

BLACKWATER
FAMILY TREE

*Note: Tommy Lee Burgess is illegitimate.

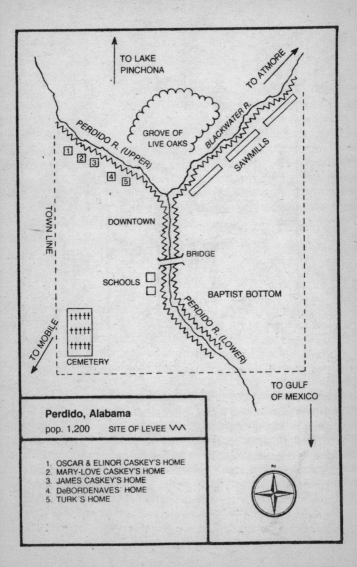

TO LAKE
PINCHONA

TO ATMORE

PERDIDO R. (UPPER)

GROVE OF
LIVE OAKS

BLACKWATER R.

SAWMILLS

1
2
3
4
5

TOWN LINE

DOWNTOWN

BRIDGE

SCHOOLS

BAPTIST BOTTOM

PERDIDO R. (LOWER)

TO MOBILE

✝✝✝✝✝
✝✝✝✝✝
✝✝✝✝✝

CEMETERY

TO GULF
OF MEXICO

N

Perdido, Alabama

pop. 1,200   SITE OF LEVEE VVV

1. OSCAR & ELINOR CASKEY'S HOME
2. MARY-LOVE CASKEY'S HOME
3. JAMES CASKEY'S HOME
4. DeBORDENAVES' HOME
5. TURK'S HOME

CHAPTER 13

~~~~~~

The Engineer

"Oh, Lord, protect us from flood, fire, maddened animals, and runaway Negroes."

That was Mary-Love Caskey's prayer before every meal, learned from her mother who had hidden silver, slaves, and chickens from the rapacity of starving Yankee marauders. But in these days, safety from a fourth danger was silently appended both in her own mind and in Sister's: *Oh, Lord, protect us from Elinor Dammert Caskey.*

Elinor, after all, was a woman to be feared. Into the well-regulated lives of the Caskeys of Perdido, Alabama, she had brought trouble and surprise. Having mysteriously appeared in the Osceola Hotel at the height of the great flood of 1919, she had cast a spell first over James Caskey—Mary-Love's brother-in-law—and then over Oscar, Mary-Love's son. She had married Oscar much against Mary-Love's desire. Elinor had hair that was the muddy red color of the Perdido River, but no family connections or financial portion. And in the end, she had taken Oscar away from Mary-Love, carried him to the house next door, and left her own child in payment for the right to take departure. *That,* Mary-Love considered, only showed Elinor to be a woman for whom no sacrifice was too great on the field of battle. She was a formidable adversary to Mary-Love, who had never before had anyone question her sovereignty.

If Mary-Love and Sister had been protective of the infant Miriam before, how close did they hold her now! Two weeks had passed since Elinor and Oscar had moved out, and as yet Elinor had shown no sign of repenting of her bargain. Mary-Love was fifty-one and would never have another child of her own. Sister was just under thirty, and had no prospects of marriage; it was unlikely she would possess a daughter other than the one her sister-in-law had given up to her. They wouldn't leave the child alone for an instant, for fear that Elinor—watching from behind one of the newly hung curtains of her back parlor— would rush over, swoop the child into her arms, and carry her back in sneaking triumph. Neither of these women intended to relinquish Miriam even though all the world and the law should demand it of them.

Mary-Love and Sister, in the beginning, had steeled themselves against what they imagined would be constant visits from Elinor. They were certain she would make suggestions for a better way to do this or that for the child, would burst into tears and beg to have Miriam for only an hour every morning, would moon over her daughter's crib, and would endlessly seek opportunities to snatch her away. But Elinor did none of those things. In fact, Elinor never came to see her daughter at all. She rocked placidly on the front porch of her new house, and corrected the pronunciation of Zaddie Sapp, who sat at her feet with a sixth-grade reader. Elinor nodded politely to Sister and Mary-Love when she saw them, or at least when it was impossible to pretend that she had *not* seen them, but she never asked to see the child. Mary-Love and Sister—who had never before been so united upon any issue whatsoever—conferred and tried to puzzle out whether Elinor ought to be trusted or not. They decided that, for safety's sake, her aloof attitude should be considered a tactic to put them off their guard. So their vigilance was maintained.

On Sundays, Mary-Love and Sister took turns staying home with the child during morning service. One or the other would sit in the same pew with Elinor, nod politely to her, and speak if the occasion allowed. But then Mary-Love suggested, as a taunt to Elinor, that she and Sister should *both* attend church. Elinor, seeing them there together, would realize that little Miriam was alone, protected only by Ivey Sapp—but she would not be able to escape the service and fetch her daughter out. Sister and Mary-Love were always careful never to leave the house on Sunday morning until they had seen Oscar and Elinor drive off to the church together, for fear that one day Elinor might remain behind and purloin her daughter before the first hymn had been sung.

One Sunday, however, Mary-Love and Sister both happened to be away from the front window when Oscar drove off. They assumed that Elinor had gone with him. At church they discovered, to their terrible dismay, that Elinor had remained at home, to tend Zaddie through the mumps. Their voices trembled through the hymns, they heard not a word of the sermon, they forgot to rise when they ought to have risen, and remained standing when they ought to have sat down again. They rushed home, and discovered Miriam sound asleep in the crib that was kept on the side porch. Ivey Sapp crooned a wordless song above her. Next door, Elinor Caskey sat on her front porch with the Mobile *Register*. Nothing in the world could have been easier than for Elinor to walk right across and up onto the porch, hold off Ivey with a stern word, lift Miriam out of her crib, and march straight back home with her. But Elinor had done no such thing.

Elinor, Sister and Mary-Love concluded, did not want her daughter back at all.

Convinced as they were that Elinor had in truth given up her daughter—though at a considerable loss to understand how she could have done such a thing—Sister and Mary-Love began to wonder what Oscar thought of the business. Oscar *did* sometimes visit his mother and sister, though he never took meals with them, and, as Sister pointed out, he never entered the house, but confined his visits to the side porch. Sometimes in the late afternoon, if he saw them on the porch, he'd come across and sit in the swing for a few minutes. He'd speak his greeting to his sister and his mother, then would lean over the crib and say, "How you, Miriam?" quite as if he expected the six-month-old child to answer him in kind. He didn't seem particularly interested in his daughter, and would merely nod and give a little smile if Sister described some surprisingly advanced or fascinatingly comical event in Miriam's development. And soon taking his leave with the excuse that Elinor would be wondering where he was and what he was doing, he would say, "So long, Mama. Bye-bye, Sister. See you later, Miriam." By the repetition of this pattern, which served only to emphasize the slightness of the hold their company and proximity held over him, Sister and Mary-Love came to understand that in gaining Miriam and jettisoning Elinor, they had also lost Oscar.

* * *

In the great new house on the town line Oscar and Elinor rattled about in their sixteen rooms. In the evening, he and Elinor sat down at the breakfast room table and ate the cold remainder of that afternoon's dinner. The kitchen door was propped open so that Zaddie, who stood at the counter and ate her own identical meal, should not feel lonely. Every other evening, when the bill changed, Oscar and Elinor went to the Ritz. Even though admission was only five cents, they always gave Zaddie a quarter to get into the colored balcony, whether she went or not. When they got home, they sat out in one of the four swings on the upstairs sleeping porch. In a bit, as Oscar desultorily rocked the swing with the toe of one shoe, Elinor would turn and lay her head in his lap. Together they would stare through the screen at the moonlit Perdido, flowing almost silently behind the house. And if Oscar talked at all, it was of his work, or of the valiant progress of the water oaks—which, after only two years of growth, were now nearly thirty feet high—or of what gossip he had heard related that morning at the barber shop.

But he never mentioned their daughter, though the window of Miriam's room was visible from where they rocked in the swing, and that window was sometimes lighted, and Mary-Love or Sister sometimes briefly appeared moving purposefully about, tending to the daughter who was as lost to him as if she had been stolen by gypsies or drowned in the river.

Elinor was again expecting a child, but it seemed to Oscar that this pregnancy was much slower than the first. His wife's belly seemed to swell less—and later in her term—and he urged her to visit Dr. Benquith. Elinor did so and returned with the report that all was well. However, she acceded to Oscar's wish that she not return to teach that fall, and rather to Oscar's surprise, Elinor seemed content to remain

13

all day in the house. Also, for propriety's sake and for Oscar's ease of mind, she gave up her morning swims in the Perdido. Nevertheless, despite his wife's precautions and Dr. Benquith's reassurances, Oscar remained unsatisfied and uneasy.

Mary-Love Caskey would have liked Perdido to acknowledge that she had won the battle with her daughter-in-law. And how could Perdido *not* think so, when Mary-Love was in possession of the spoils? Even if baby Miriam had been won at the expense of her son's affection, Oscar was bound to have gone off somewhere, with someone, sooner or later. Besides, what son ever remained permanently estranged from his mother? There was no question in Mary-Love's mind but that Oscar would someday return to her, and then her conquest of Elinor Caskey would be sweet and complete indeed!

But Perdido, to Mary-Love's consternation, didn't see things that way at all. What Perdido saw was that when the smoke had cleared, Elinor Caskey was sitting at the top of the hill, waving an untattered and unbloodied flag. She had given up her only child, but from all appearances she didn't seem to care one way or the other.

And more importantly, Elinor Caskey wasn't acting like a defeated woman. If she never paid visits to her mother-in-law and her sister-in-law and her abandoned daughter, in public she was never anything other than pleasant and friendly to them. Nothing in her tone savored of irony or sarcasm or the heaping-on of burning coals; she was never heard to speak a word against either Mary-Love or Sister. Nor had she sought to suborn Caroline DeBordenave or Manda Turk into rebellion against Mary-Love by establishing an intimacy either with the women themselves or with their daughters.

Elinor never objected to Oscar's visits to his

14

mother's house, and never made him feel guilty about having gone. She sent Zaddie over with boxes of peaches and bottles of blackberry nectar she had put up herself. But she never once set foot in Mary-Love's house and never asked after her daughter's health and never invited Mary-Love or Sister over to see what the new house looked like all furnished and decorated.

Thus, once convinced that there was to be no attempt to reappropriate Miriam, Mary-Love decided that Elinor had not been sufficiently humbled, and began to look about for a way to crush her daughter-in-law.

A year and a half before, on the day after Elinor had announced her first pregnancy, there had arrived in Perdido a man called Early Haskew. He was thirty years of age, with brown hair and brown eyes and a thick brown mustache. He had a sunburned complexion, strong arms and long legs, and a wardrobe that seemed to consist entirely of khaki trousers and white shirts. He had gone to school at the University of Alabama, and had been superficially wounded on the bank of the Marne. And he had learned, during his tenure in France, everything there was to know about earthworks. Earth, in fact, seemed to pervade his consciousness, and he was never really comfortable except with both his large feet firmly planted on solid ground. There seemed, moreover, always to be earth beneath his fingernails and in the creases of his sunburned skin; but no one looking at him ever thought this attributable to a relaxation of personal hygiene. The dirt seemed only to be a part of the man, and wholly unobjectionable. He was an engineer, and he had come to Perdido to see whether it might be possible to protect the town from future flooding by the construction of a series

15

of levees along the banks of the Perdido and Black-water rivers.

With the help of two surveying students from Auburn Polytechnic, Early Haskew plotted out the town, plumbed the depths of the rivers, measured heights above sea level, examined records at the town hall, and noted the fading high-water marks left by the flood of 1919. He talked with the foremen of the mills who used the rivers for the transport of logs, took photographs of the sections of town that lay near the banks of the rivers, dispatched letters of enquiry to engineers in Natchez and New Orleans, and drew a salary that was, unbeknownst to any but members of the town council, paid entirely by James Caskey. At the end of eight weeks, during which he seemed to be everywhere, with his maps, instruments, notebooks, cameras, pencils, and assistants, Early Haskew disappeared. He had promised detailed plans within three months, but James Caskey received a letter a short time after his departure, announcing his inability to meet that deadline, owing to some army work required of him over at Camp Rucca. Early Haskew was still in the reserves.

But now he was finished with the reserves, and was returning to Perdido with the intention of completing his plans as quickly as possible. Who knew how soon the waters might rise again?

Early Haskew had lived with his mother in a tiny town called Pine Cone, on the edge of the Alabama Wiregrass area. She had died recently, and Early had seen no necessity of returning to Pine Cone. He sold his mother's house, and wrote to James Caskey asking if the millowner would be so kind as to find him a place to live. Early hoped not only to provide the plans but to supervise the building of the levee—if the town council were pleased to judge him fit for the work—so he might be in town for as long as two years. And two years was enough time to justify the purchase of a house.

James Caskey mentioned this news at Mary-Love's one evening. James had thought it a piece of information of interest, but of not much importance, so he was startled by the vehemence with which Mary-Love Caskey seized upon it.

"Oh, James," she cried, "don't you let that man buy a house!"

"Why not?" said James mildly. "If he wants it, and he has the money?"

"Wasting his money!" said Mary-Love.

"Well, what do you want the man to do, Mama?" asked Sister, who was sitting sideways in her chair at the table and bouncing Miriam up and down on her knee while nine-year-old Grace, sitting beside her, held out a finger for the baby to hold for balance and security.

"I don't want him to waste his money," said Mary-Love. "I want him to come here and stay with us. We have that extra room that used to be Oscar's. It's got a private bathroom and a sitting room he can set up a drafting table in. I think I might go out and get one of those tables myself," she mused, or appeared to muse. "I have always wanted one."

"You have not," said Sister, contradicting her mother as she might have said, "Pass the peas, please."

"I have!"

"Mary-Love, why do you want Mr. Haskew staying here?" asked James.

"Because Sister and I are lonely, and Mr. Haskew needs a place to stay. He doesn't want to live all by himself. Who'd cook for him? Who'd wash his clothes? He's a nice man. We had him over to dinner one day when he was here before, remember? James, write to that man and tell him he can stay here in this nice big house with us."

"He ate his peas on a knife," added Sister. "Mama, you said you had never seen a decent man do that in public. You wondered what kind of home he came from. I was the only one in this house who was nice to him. One evening Mr. Haskew came by to speak to Oscar, and Elinor got right up out of the chair and walked away and wouldn't even let herself be introduced to him. Never saw anything so rude in my life."

"Why do you suppose she did that?" asked James, who now suddenly had an inkling what Mary-Love's energetic and unexpected proposal was all about.

"I don't know," said Mary-Love quickly. "What I *do* want to know is, are you gone write that letter, James, or am I?"

James shrugged, though he didn't know what was to come of it. "I'll write it tomorrow at the office—"

"Why not tonight?"

"Mary-Love, how do you know that that man's gone say yes? He may not *want* to live here."

"Why wouldn't he?" demanded Mary-Love.

"Well," said James after a moment, "maybe he wouldn't want to be in the house with a tiny baby, that cries."

"Miriam doesn't cry," said Sister indignantly.

"I know she doesn't," returned James, "but babies tend to, and you cain't expect Early Haskew to realize he's dealing with a special case here."

"Well, you tell him he is," said Mary-Love, and James agreed to write the letter that very night.

"And James," said Mary-Love in a whisper as she saw her brother-in-law out the door that evening, "one more thing. Not a word to Oscar about this and not a word to Elinor, either. I want it all set up before we say anything—I want it all to be such a surprise!"

CHAPTER 14

Plans and Predictions

Early Haskew received letters from both Mary-Love Caskey and her brother-in-law, James, offering the hospitality of Mary-Love's home and Mary-Love's table for the duration of the engineer's stay in Perdido. Early wrote back a roughly worded but polite refusal, stating that he did not wish to take advantage of the town and the one family in particular that was to provide him lucrative employment for an extended period of time. Two more letters were fired off; James stating that Mary-Love's offer was made wholly without prejudice or prompting and that—since no house was available to purchase—it would be a solution that seemed best all around, and Mary-Love complaining that she had just purchased a drafting table and what on earth was she to do with *that* if Early Haskew took up residence in the Osceola Hotel. Weakened by this second volley, Early Haskew made a polite capitulation. The surrendered man, however, insisted upon paying ten dollars a week for his room and board.

The engineer came to Perdido in March 1922. Bray Sugarwhite fetched him in Mary-Love's automobile from the Atmore station, and he arrived at Mary-Love's house in time for dinner that Wednesday afternoon.

Sister was immediately shy about the man, who was large and handsome and unselfconscious in a way that was not at all characteristic of the male population of Perdido. Early Haskew was certainly different from Oscar, who was quiet and—in his way—subtle. And the man seemed nothing at all like James, whose quietness and greater subtlety were distinctly tinged by femininity. There was nothing quiet or subtle or feminine about Early Haskew. At dinner that night, his plate was several times nearly upset onto the tablecloth, he rattled his silverware, tea sloshed out of his glass, his napkin was in use constantly. Three times Ivey was called to replace his fork that had dropped, again, to the floor. When he mentioned, in the course of conversation, that his mother had been almost stone-deaf, his habit of speaking loudly and of overenunciating his words seemed satisfactorily accounted for. He also explained that he had come by his unusual Christian name from the fact that his mother had been born an Early, in Fairfax County, Virginia. With all his large gestures, and the little accidents that befell him at the table, he made the room seem a little small for comfort, as if the giant in a circus sideshow had been compelled to take up residence in the little people's caravan.

In Sister's memory, such a man had never before been found at Mary-Love's table. Mary-Love Caskey was genteel to the points of her teeth. Sister wondered at her mother's forbearance of Early's gaucheries, and at Mary-Love's sincere hospitality toward the engineer. "I hope, Mr. Haskew," said Mary-Love with a smile that might have been described only as gleeful, "that you intend to save me and my family from the floodwaters."

"I intend to do just that, Miz Caskey," replied Early Haskew in a voice that would have reached her had she been sitting at the table in Elinor's house. "That's why I'm here. And I sure do like my room upstairs. I just wish you hadn't gone to the expense of that drafting table!"

"If that drafting table can save us from another flood, it's gone be worth every penny I spent on it. Besides, I don't believe you would have come to live with us if I hadn't had that thing ready waiting."

After dinner, when James had returned to the mill and Mary-Love and Sister and Early were sitting on the porch with glasses of tea, they noticed Zaddie Sapp passing by, evidently off on some errand for Elinor. Quickly, and in a low voice, Mary-Love said, "Sister, tell Zaddie to come up on the porch for a minute."

Zaddie rather wondered at the summons, for she was Elinor's acknowledged creature and as such hardly welcome in Mary-Love's house—or even on that porch. Zaddie still raked Mary-Love's yard every morning, but Mary-Love could scarcely bring herself to nod a greeting to the twelve-year-old.

"Hey, Zaddie," said Mary-Love, "come on inside. There's somebody I want you to meet."

Zaddie came through the screen door and onto the side porch. She stared at Early Haskew, and he stared at her.

"Zaddie," said Mary-Love, "this is Early Haskew. This is the man who's gone save Perdido from the next flood."

"Ma'am?"

"Mr. Haskew is gone build a levee to save Perdido!"

"Yes, ma'am," said Zaddie politely.

"How you do, Zaddie?" shouted Early Haskew, and Zaddie blinked at the force of his voice.

"I'm fine, Mr. Skew."

"Haskew, Zaddie," corrected Sister.

"I'm fine," repeated Zaddie.

"Thank Mr. Haskew, Zaddie, for saving you from the next flood," instructed Mary-Love.

"Thank you, sir," said Zaddie obediently.

"You're welcome, Zaddie."

Zaddie and Early Haskew looked at each other in some puzzlement, for neither had any idea why this meeting should have been brought about. Zaddie wondered why she had been called over to be introduced to a white man when only that morning she had been shooed away when she tried to peek into Miriam's carriage. And Early wondered if it were Mary-Love's intention to introduce him to every man, woman, and child—white and colored and Indian—whose life and property would be protected by the levee he intended to build around the town.

Sister thought she had the answer. In the dissemination of information Zaddie was as efficient as a telegraph, and Elinor would learn of Early Haskew's presence in Mary-Love's house as surely as if a Western Union man came to the door and handed over the message in a yellow envelope.

Mary-Love said to Zaddie, "We have kept you, child. Weren't you on an errand for Elinor?"

"Yes, ma'am," replied Zaddie. "I got to go fetch some paraffin."

"Then go do it," said Mary-Love, and Zaddie ran away.

Mary-Love turned to Early and said, "Zaddie belongs to Elinor and Oscar. You've met my son."

"Yes, ma'am."

"But you haven't met his wife Elinor, my daughter-in-law?"

"No, ma'am."

"I suppose you will," said Mary-Love offhandedly. "I hope you have the chance, that is. They live next door in that big white house. I built that house for them as a wedding present."

"It's a fine house!"

"I know it. But you'll see, Mr. Haskew, when you've been here a little longer, that there's not much back-and-forthing between these two houses."

"No, ma'am," said Early Haskew politely, quite as if he understood all about it.

"Well..." said Mary-Love hesitantly, then abruptly concluded, "that's all."

The town council meeting that evening was attended not only by the directly elected members of the board—Oscar, Henry Turk, Dr. Leo Benquith, and three other men—but also by James Caskey and Tom DeBordenave as vitally interested parties and as millowners. Before these men Early Haskew presented a rough plan, timetable, and schedule of expenses for the construction of the levees.

The levee was to be in three parts. The largest and most substantial portion would be raised on either side of the Perdido below the junction. This would protect downtown and the area of mill workers' houses to the west of the river and Baptist Bottom to the east. The bridge over the Perdido just below the Osceola Hotel would be widened and raised to the height of the levee, and gentle approach ramps constructed. In large measure, this was a municipal levee, for it protected the greater part of residential and commercial Perdido. A second levee, half a mile long and connecting with the first, would be raised on the southern bank of the

Blackwater River, which came from the northeast of town from its source in the cypress swamp. This levee would protect the three sawmills. The third portion of the levee was shortest of all; it would run along the southern bank of the Perdido above the junction, and would protect the five homes belonging to Henry Turk, Tom DeBordenave, James Caskey, Mary-Love Caskey, and Oscar Caskey. This levee would end a hundred yards or so beyond the town line. When the rivers rose again, as was bound to happen in the course of things, the levees would protect the town, and only the uninhabited lowlands directly south of Perdido, along the course of the river, would be flooded.

In four months, Early would have detailed plans. Construction of the levee could begin immediately thereafter. The work would take at least fifteen months for the double levee along the lower Perdido, and six months each for the secondary levees. The cost he estimated to be about one million one hundred thousand dollars, a sum which momentarily staggered the town council.

Early sat back for the remainder of the meeting while the leaders of Perdido thrashed out the question. In 1919 the town had lost considerably more than the projected cost of the levee. If the town grew and the mills cut down more trees and produced more lumber, Perdido stood to lose even more in a subsequent flood. Therefore, if the money could be in any way procured, the levee ought to be built. James and Oscar, agreeing by a simple nod between them, offered to pay Early's expenses while he made up detailed plans for the levee. This would be the Caskeys' contribution to the town that had fostered them. Thus authorized and encouraged to forge ahead, Early took his leave of the meeting.

After the engineer had left, and many had said how highly they thought of the man, the leading citizens examined Early's figures again and determined that the municipal levee would cost seven hundred thousand dollars, the levee along the Blackwater would cost two hundred and fifty thousand, and the levee along the upper Perdido, behind the millowners' homes, would be one hundred and fifty thousand. The millowners, in separate conference, decided that they should bear the cost of the levee behind their own homes and that they should split with the town the cost of the levee that protected the mills. This lowered the town's burden to eight hundred and twenty-five thousand dollars, and that at least *sounded* a good deal better than one million one hundred thousand.

James agreed to drive to Bay Minette and call upon the Baldwin County legislator to see what could be done about a bond issue through the state government. Tom DeBordenave would talk to the banks in Mobile.

At all events, everyone felt better after the meeting. The flood of 1919 had been so disastrous, so unexpected, and the town had been so unprepared, even this first step toward protection seemed like a great deal to the town council. They imagined what it would be to have the levees in place. The waters of the Perdido and the Blackwater might rise high against Early Haskew's earthworks, but Perdido children, with sunny faces, would play at skip-rope and marbles on dry earth that was far below the level of the dark, swirling water lapping ominously on the other side.

That evening, while Oscar was at the meeting of the town council, Elinor sat with her sewing on the upstairs porch. Zaddie joined her there, and told about the strange thing that had happened to her that afternoon at Miss Mary-Love's.

"Why she want me to meet that man?" asked Zaddie curiously and with complete confidence that Elinor would be able to supply the answer.

Elinor had put down her sewing. Her mouth had tightened. She stood and went over to the porch railing. Her pregnant belly created only a little sway and awkwardness in her purposeful walk. "Don't you know, Zaddie?"

"No, ma'am."

Elinor turned and with barely suppressed anger said, "She wanted you to meet that man so you would come back here and tell me about it, that's why!"

"Ma'am?"

"Zaddie, you know Miss Mary-Love won't give me the time of day—"

"No, ma'am!" agreed Zaddie emphatically, as if that state of affairs had been reached only through some cunning stratagem of Elinor's.

"—but she wanted me to know that *that man* was back in town."

"You mean, Mr. Skew?"

Elinor nodded grimly.

"Why Miss Mary-Love want you to know that?"

"Because she knows how much I hate Early Haskew, that's why. She did it to perturb my mind, Zaddie. And I'll tell you something, it *does* perturb my mind!"

"Why?"

"Zaddie, don't you know? Don't you have any idea?"

"No, ma'am."

"You know what that man wants to do? He wants to dam up the rivers. He wants to build levees all around this town to keep the rivers from flooding."

"Miss El'nor, we don't want no more floods," said Zaddie cautiously. "Do we?"

"There aren't going to be any more floods," said Elinor emphatically.

26

"Ivey say there might be. Ivey say it all depend on the squirrels."

"Ivey doesn't know what she's talking about," said Elinor. "Ivey doesn't know anything about floods." She paced quickly back and forth along the long porch railing glancing now at Mary-Love's house, now at her splendid grove of water oaks, but staring mostly down at the muddy red Perdido flowing swiftly and silently behind the house. Zaddie stood quite still with one raised hand grasping the swing chain as she watched Miss Elinor.

"None of them knows about floods or anything about the rivers, Zaddie. You'd think they'd have learned something, wouldn't you, living so long around here, where every time they look out the window they see the Perdido flowing by, where every time they go to work or go to the store they have to cross a bridge and see the water flowing under it, where they catch their fish for supper on Saturday night, where their oldest children get baptized, and where their youngest children drown. You'd think they'd know something by now, wouldn't you, Zaddie?"

"Yes, ma'am," said Zaddie quietly, but Miss Elinor did not even turn around to look at the black girl.

"They don't though," said Elinor bitterly. "They don't know anything. They're going to hire *that man* to build levees, they're going to pretend that the rivers aren't there anymore. And, Zaddie, Miss Mary-Love's going to see to help this project along, even if she has to take money out of her own purse to do it. And do you know why?"

"Why?"

"To spite me. That's why she's doing it, and for no other reason in the world. Lord, that woman despises me!" Elinor turned suddenly back, strode forward and threw herself into the swing. She looked at Zaddie, who had seated herself cautiously

27

in the swing beside Elinor. With one swift kick Elinor propelled the swing into motion. She pressed both hands against her belly, and when she spoke her words seemed to join in rhythm with the jerking chain.

"Zaddie, do you know what we're going to see a few months from now when we sit in this swing?"

"No, ma'am. What?"

"We're going to be looking at a pile of dirt. *That man* is going to block our view of the river with a pile of dirt. And Mary-Love is going to be out there with a shovel helping. She'll do it to make me mad. And she'll put a shovel in Sister's hands. And she'll have Miriam out there in a baby carriage, and she'll lean over and she'll say to Miriam, 'Oh, you watch, child, you watch me ruin your mama's view! You watch me raise up earth in front of your real mama's eyes!' Oh, I hate it, Zaddie! I hate it all like hell!"

Elinor rocked in the swing and stared out at the Perdido. Her breath was harsh and uneven.

"Miss El'nor, can I ask you a question?" said Zaddie timidly.

"What?"

"What if they don't put up the levee? Won't there be another flood? Sometime, I mean? Miss El'nor, people died in that flood!"

Elinor put her foot down sharply and the swing stopped with a jerk, nearly pitching Zaddie out onto the floor. Elinor turned and looked directly into the black girl's face.

"Zaddie, you listen to me. That levee—if it ever gets built—is not going to do this town one bit of good."

"What you mean?"

"I mean that while I am alive and while I am living in this house, whether there's a levee or not

28

there will be no flood in Perdido. The rivers will not rise."

"Miss El'nor, you cain't—"

Elinor ignored the protest. "But, Zaddie, when I am dead—whether there's a levee or not—this town and everybody in it will be washed off the face of the earth..."

CHAPTER 15

The Baptism

When Zaddie went to Elinor with news of the arrival in town of Early Haskew she had not known that this man was to live in the house right next door. Mary-Love would have given much to see Elinor's face when she learned that Early was to sleep in the bed in the room that Elinor herself had occupied not so many months before. Oscar, not anticipating his wife's reaction, had mentioned this only in passing that evening. The following evening Oscar and his wife were walking past Mary-Love's house on the way to the Ritz and saw Early sitting on the porch with Sister. Elinor stopped in her tracks, turned and marched home, and wouldn't speak a single word to Oscar for the rest of the night. She strung a hammock on the upstairs porch and slept within sight of the river.

Calmer next morning at the breakfast table, she said to Oscar, "Your mama wants me to lose this baby."

Oscar raised his eyes in astonishment. "Elinor, what do you mean to say!"

"I mean to say Miss Mary-Love wants me to miscarry. She wants Miriam to be an only child so she can lord Miriam over me and you."

Oscar had never before heard Elinor speak of their daughter, and now that she had, he was dumbfounded by the perversity of her attitude.

"Elinor," he said earnestly, "that is just wrong. Why would you think a horrible thing like that?"

"There is no other reason for her to have asked *that man* into her house."

"Mr. Haskew?"

"That man is sleeping in *your* room, Oscar."

"I know it. And I think Mama is doing a fine thing. I think she looks on it as something she is doing for the benefit of Perdido, providing a pleasant place for Mr. Haskew to do his drawings. Did you know she bought him a table that put her back sixty-five dollars? And a chair with a swivel seat that was fifteen dollars more? Mama was looking out for Mr. Haskew's well-being."

Elinor turned away and stared out the window at Mary-Love's house. "It just makes me ill to sit here and look at that house and to know *that man* is sitting inside it with a pencil and a ruler, drawing up the levee."

Oscar thought he began to understand. "Now, I sort of remembered that you didn't take to Mr. Haskew when he was here a year or so ago—"

Elinor looked at her husband with a countenance that seemed to say, *That is an Alabama understatement.*

"—but I thought it was just because you didn't take to *him,* you know, the way I don't take to okra.

32

But it wasn't, was it? It was just because he was coming here to build the levee, and you don't like the levee."

"That's right. I don't like the levee, Oscar. This town doesn't need it. There won't be any more floods."

"Elinor, you just cain't be sure of that. We cain't afford to take chances. Even if I were sure nobody was gone die, I'd try to push it through. Do you know how much lumber we lost in 1919? Do you know how much *money* we lost? And we were lucky. Poor old Tom DeBordenave hasn't recovered yet, and I'm not sure he ever will. That flood could come again next year, and then if *any* of us recovered I'd be mighty surprised."

"There won't be any high water next year," said Elinor calmly.

Oscar regarded his wife with a baffled face. "Elinor," he said at last, "you just cain't let Mr. Haskew upset you. He is a very nice man and I'm sure he doesn't want to hear that he is distressing a pregnant woman in the next house over."

"Miss Mary-Love did this on purpose," Elinor repeated.

They were back where they had begun. Oscar sighed, got up from the table, and prepared to leave for work. He knew that Elinor's view was as distorted as the image of an object observed through ten feet of flowing river water. But that afternoon when he dropped by his mother's house on the way home, in the middle of a discussion about how things were going at the mill, Mary-Love said, "Oscar, does Elinor know that Mr. Haskew has taken up residence here with us?"

"She knows it," said Oscar shortly. After the sudden introduction of a new subject into the coversation, it was best to say as little as possible in reply.

A man never knew what someone wanted to get out of him.

"Well, what did she say?"

That river water wasn't flowing as quickly anymore. Oscar was beginning to see what rested on the shifting bed so far below the surface.

"She didn't say much, Mama. Elinor doesn't think this town needs a levee. Elinor doesn't think there's going to be another flood. So I suppose she thinks that Mr. Haskew is wasting his time and that we are wasting our money."

Mary-Love snorted in contempt. "What does Elinor know about floods and levees? What does Elinor know about people's houses and businesses getting washed away in rising water?"

"Well," Oscar pointed out, "she got trapped by the water. If you recall, Bray and I found her stranded in the Osceola Hotel."

Mary-Love said nothing, but her face was so expressive of the delicate wish that Elinor Dammert had remained stranded until she starved or perished of damp ennui that Oscar responded as if the remark had been made aloud. "Mama, if I hadn't rescued Elinor and then married her, you wouldn't have Miriam."

"That is true," admitted Mary-Love. "I will always be grateful to Elinor for giving me her little girl. Her first child. She didn't have to do it. So, Elinor didn't say anything about Mr. Haskew? Did you tell her we had given Mr. Haskew your old room? And that he is sleeping in the bed that she gave birth in?"

Oscar was surprised into silence for a few moments. He was shocked that his mother had given herself away so easily. He could see quite clearly through the river water now, and he realized that Elinor had understood from the beginning. Mary-Love's invitation to Early Haskew *had* been made precisely to aggravate Elinor, though Oscar wasn't convinced that Mary-Love was seeking to induce a miscarriage. The acknowledgment of this meanness in his mother—there was no other word for it—turned Oscar firmly to his wife's side on the issue. He would have had his tongue ripped out of his throat rather than say to Mary-Love that Elinor was distressed by the proximity of the engineer. In fact, he went so far as actually to mislead his mother by remarking, "Elinor is glad you've got somebody to keep you company. She figures you may have been lonely since we moved. That house is so big, Mama, and it takes so much time and effort just to keep it going that Elinor doesn't get over here as much as she would like."

Mary-Love looked uncertainly at her son—whose face was quite blandly pleasant—as if she were trying to determine whether or not he was playing a role, or whether he spoke—as men in Perdido, and probably men everywhere, tended to speak—without any regard for the effect of his words.

At supper that evening Oscar told Elinor exactly what he had said to his mother, and Elinor, listening to that straightforward recital, had no doubt that Oscar understood the importance of his speech. She gave him far more credit than did his mother. Elinor smiled and said, "See what I told you, Oscar?"

"You were right about Mama, though I wouldn't have thought it of her. But, Elinor, I have got to say..."

"Say what?"

"That I am gone be supporting Mr. Haskew in his work. I think there's gone be another flood sooner or later, and I think the levees are gone have to be built. I know you don't like it, but I have got to do all I can to protect this town and the mills."

"All right, Oscar," said Elinor with surprising calmness. "You have started to see some things cor-

times Bray drove him out deep into Baldwin and Escambia counties to look over quarries of various sorts. He'd come back covered with mud. After he'd bathed and changed clothes, bits of red Alabama clay were still wedged in the creases of his face and beneath the nails of his large hands. Miriam loved him, and in the evening he'd bounce her up and down on his knee to her delight for as long as she wanted it.

Because of him, commerce between Mary-Love's and Oscar's houses very nearly ceased altogether. There were no more small gifts of fruits or preserves sent over with Zaddie; Oscar did not come as frequently as formerly. Even the sisters Zaddie and Ivey seemed to have dissolved their kinship. Mary-Love satisfied herself with the thought that she had embedded a large thorn in the side of her daughter-in-law. One day, seeking to probe that wound, Mary-Love remarked to her son, "Oscar, we don't see much of Elinor anymore. Is she doing all right? We have been worried."

Oscar replied, "Well, Mama, it's getting 'long about that time, you know, and it wouldn't do for Elinor to tire herself out with constant visiting. In fact," he joked, "I keep her locked in her room all the time now. I have Zaddie standing outside the door, reading to her through the keyhole."

Oscar said this in order to deprive his mother of the satisfaction of any information about just how upset Elinor continued to be. But what he said regarding his wife's pregnancy was quite true; it *was* getting along about that time. In fact, by Oscar's casual calculation, the baby—Elinor still hadn't told him whether it was to be a boy or a girl—was already overdue.

But overdue or not, the baby held off another four weeks. Oscar became truly worried. Elinor was not feeling very well and she took to her bed. Dr. Ben-

rectly, but you don't see everything right yet. The
time will come when you will learn the error of your
ways...."

Mary-Love had at first considered Early Haskew
merely a goad to her daughter-in-law, but he quickly
came to be more than that. He was a pleasant man,
kind and gentle, and she soon grew used to his loud
voice and his habit of eating peas with a knife. His
countrified roughness wasn't totally unpleasant in
a man so young and handsome, even though Mary-
Love was certain that passing years would coarsen
Early. Sister, too—or rather Sister, especially—
liked him, for she had never spent any time at all
around a man who wasn't close family.

Early sat in his sitting room all day working at
the drafting table. Sister supplied him with cups of
coffee and her own cookies. When the day was hot
she got him iced tea, and when there wasn't anything
more that she could get for him she went quietly into
his room with a book and sat in a chair turned toward
his profile.

"You worry him!" cried Mary-Love.

"I do not!" protested Sister. And if she did, he
showed no sign of it. He must have said thank you
to Sister eighty times a day, and that thank you was
always cordial and sincere. When Mary-Love insisted that Sister leave the engineer alone and sit with
her on the side porch with another quilt that they
were piecing together, Sister fidgeted until Mary-
Love gave reluctant consent for her to return to her
place beside Early's drafting board.

Occasionally, when he said his eyes were weary,
he'd come down and sit on the porch with Sister and
Mary-Love and rock in the swing with his eyes closed
and talk in a moderate voice. He went for long walks
about town, particularly along the banks of the rivers, looking at soil and formations of clay. Other

quith came to examine her and afterward he told Oscar, "She's in discomfort."

"Yes, but is the baby all right?"

"It's kicking. I felt it."

"Well, tell me, is it gone be a boy or a girl?"

Leo Benquith looked strangely at Oscar, and didn't reply for a moment.

"I bet this one's gone be a boy," said Oscar. "Am I right?"

"Oscar," said Dr. Benquith slowly, "you know, don't you, that there's no way in the world to tell if it's gone be a boy or a girl?"

Oscar looked puzzled for a moment, then replied, "Well, you know, that's what I used to think. I mean, that's what I had always heard. But Elinor knows— I *know* she knows—she just won't tell me."

"Your wife has been manipulating one of your lower extremities, Oscar."

Oscar's curiosity was soon satisfied, for on the nineteenth of May, 1922, Elinor gave birth to a five-pound girl.

The doctor had left, and Roxie was downstairs washing the bloody linen, when Oscar said to Elinor, "Did you know it was gone be a girl?"

"Of course I did."

"Why didn't you tell me?"

"I didn't want you to be disappointed." She held out the baby for Oscar's inspection. "You probably wanted a boy, Oscar, but I knew once you had seen this little girl you would love her to death! That's why I didn't tell you."

"I do love her to death! I would have loved her anyway!"

"Well, then," said Elinor softly, putting the infant to her breast, "I was wrong about it. Next time I *will* tell you."

There was a sort of state visit that afternoon by

Mary-Love and Sister. Sister carried Miriam in her arms, and Oscar reflected somewhat uncomfortably that this was the first time his firstborn daughter had ever been inside her parents' house. After having peered curiously into all the rooms on the way up, exclaiming softly and disparagingly on what they saw, Sister and Mary-Love entered Elinor's bedroom and stood on opposite sides of the bed. As if at a prearranged signal, they bent down together and kissed Elinor on either cheek. Elinor pulled back the corner of the blanket that was wrapped about her new daughter, and said, "See? Now I've got one of my own." She looked at her first daughter, still in Sister's arms, and said, "Miriam, this is your sister Frances."

"Is that what we are calling her?" said Oscar.

"Yes," replied Elinor, then added after a moment, "it was my mother's name."

"It's a real pretty name," said Mary-Love. "Elinor, Sister and I don't want to tire you out, so listen, if there's anything you need, you just send Zaddie over, and we will drop everything and go out and get it."

"I thank you, Miss Mary-Love. Thank you, Sister."

"Mama, we ought to go. Early's gone wonder what became of us."

At the mention of the engineer's name, Elinor's polite smile froze. She didn't say another word to Sister or Mary-Love.

That night, while Elinor—remarkably recovered—was walking around and around the nursery with Frances, singing to the baby and holding it out to stare at it and make faces at it and grin at it and drawing it back in again to kiss and fondle, Oscar performed calculations on the birth of his daughter that weren't so casual. He worked back nine months from this date of Frances' birth—Leo Benquith had told him that the delivery and the pregnancy had been normal in every respect—and came up with August 19, 1921.

That was the date they had moved into the new house. He certainly remembered that he and Elinor had made love that night, for it had been the first time in their own home—but what he also remembered, with not a little uneasiness, was that that was also the date on which, earlier in the evening, Elinor had *announced* her pregnancy.

The night of the birth of Frances Caskey, Elinor declared her intention of remaining in the nursery with her new daughter. Pleased that his wife was showing such interest and delight in her new child, in such sharp contrast to her treatment of Miriam, Oscar eagerly acquiesced. He lay in bed a long while, unable to fall asleep, thinking of Elinor, the pregnancy, and the peculiar coincidence of dates.

Next door, in Mary-Love's house, Early Haskew snored louder than he talked. Mary-Love tossed in her bed, pondering what effect the birth of Frances might have on things, fearing that the child might be the means by which Elinor gained an ascendancy acknowledged all over Perdido. And in her room, Sister thought alternately of Miriam, whom she loved very dearly, and of the man snoring in the room at the end of the hall, to whom she was not indifferent. Beside Sister in the bed, little Miriam Caskey dreamed her formless dreams of nameless things to eat and nameless things to pick up and nameless things to hide in the little box that Mary-Love had given her.

And in the next house, Grace Caskey tossed and turned and didn't even want to go to sleep, so excited was she by the birth of Frances. Grace envisioned a trio of cousins—herself, Miriam, and Frances—loyal and loving. James Caskey thought—or did he dream?—of the earth above his wife's grave, and wondered whether it ought not to be planted over in verbena or phlox. Eventually all the Caskeys fell asleep, and all dreamed of whatever concerned them most.

That night while the Caskeys slept and dreamed, fog roiled up out of the Perdido River and spilled across the dry Caskey property.

Fogs were not uncommon in this part of Alabama, but they came only at night and were seen by few. This fog, thicker and darker than usual, rose up out of the river as a beast of prey rises up in the night after a long diurnal sleep, keen to slake its hunger. It wrapped itself around the Caskey houses, enveloping them in a silent, thick, unmoving mist. What before had been only dark was now black. It was so silent, so subtle, that its arrival waked no one at all. The river moisture pervaded the houses and surrounded the sleepers with a suffocating dampness. Even Early Haskew's snoring was muffled. Yet still none of the Caskeys woke, and if they struggled against it, they did so only in their dreams, dreams in which the oppressive fog had arms and legs that were slick and damp, and a mouth that exhaled mist and night.

Zaddie Sapp was the only one to know of it. She dreamed of the fog, dreamed that its moist fingers pulled back the sheet from her cot so that she grew chill, and dreamed that the fog awakened her and beckoned her to come out from the protection of her tiny closet behind the kitchen. The dream was so convincing that Zaddie opened her eyes to prove to herself that the fog was not there. But when she did so, and looked straight up at the ceiling, Zaddie saw thick wisps of the mist floating in her window. At the same time, very soft and muffled, she heard the sodden creek of the hinges of the lattice-door at the back of the house. At first she disbelieved her ears, the sound seemed so distant. Then she heard a step upon the stairs that led down to the back yard.

She sat up suddenly, and wisps of fog swirled into sudden turbulence before her eyes. Zaddie wasn't afraid of thieves, because nothing had been stolen in Perdido since "Railroad" Bill held up the Turk's mill in 1883, but with trepidation she peered out the window. Little could be seen through the fog, but when she squinted she could just make out a dark form moving carefully down those steps.

Zaddie knew that it was Elinor.

One step creaked. The form paused. Zaddie perceived that Elinor carried something in her cradled arms, and what did cradled arms usually hold but a baby?

Night air and fog just couldn't be good for a child that wasn't yet a day old! Clad only in her nightgown, and without thinking to put on shoes, Zaddie jumped quietly out of the bed, opened the door of her little closet, and stepped out to the latticed back porch. She pushed open the back door, softly but without trying to disguise the fact that she was there. She stood on the back steps, and shut the door behind her.

Elinor was off in the yard ahead, nearly invisible in the fog.

"Miss El'nor," said Zaddie softly.

"Zaddie, go back inside." Elinor's voice sounded dreamy and moist. It seemed to come from a great distance.

Zaddie hesitated. "Miss El'nor, what you doing out here with that precious baby?"

Elinor shifted the child in her arms. "I'm going to baptize her in the Perdido water, and I don't need you to help. So you go back inside, you hear? A little girl like you could get lost in this fog and die!"

Elinor's voice faded, as did her shape. She was lost in the fog. Zaddie ran forward, fearful for the safety of the infant. "Miss El'nor!" Zaddie whispered in the inky darkness.

No answer came.

Zaddie ran forward toward the river. She tripped over the exposed root of one of the clumps of water oaks, and sprawled in the sand. She scrambled to her feet, and through a momentary thinning of the fog, could make out Miss Elinor's form at the edge of the water.

She again hurried forward, and grabbed her mistress's nightdress.

"Zaddie," said Elinor, her voice still distant and strange, "I told you to stay back."

"Miss El'nor, you cain't put that child in the water!"

Elinor laughed. "Do you think this river is going to hurt *my* little girl?" And with that, Elinor flung her newborn daughter into the swirling black current of the Perdido. She might have been a fisherman tossing a too-small catch back into the river.

Zaddie had long been fearful of the Perdido, knowing how many people had drowned in its unabating currents. She had heard Ivey's stories of what lived on the riverbed, and what things hid in the mud. But despite her fear, despite the fact that it was night and that the night was filled with fog, Zaddie rushed into the water in hope of saving the infant that, incredibly, had been tossed in by its mother.

"Zaddie," cried Elinor, "come back. You'll drown!"

Zaddie caught the child—or at least thought she caught it. Reaching down into the water, she had scooped up *something*. It felt very little like a baby! It was so slippery and unsoft, yet rubbery—a fishlike thing—that she very nearly let it go again. Zaddie shuddered with repulsion for whatever it was that she held in her hands, but she raised it up above the surface. She saw that she had caught hold of something black and vile, with a neckless head attached directly to a thick body. A stubby tail that was almost as thick as the body twitched convulsively, and the thing was covered with river slime. In the air it struggled to get away, to return to its element. But Zaddie held it tight, closing her fingers into its disgusting flesh. From its fishy mouth emerged a stream of foamy water, and the thrashing tail smacked against Zaddie's forearms; dull, bulging eyes shone up into her face.

Elinor's hand closed over Zaddie's shoulder.

The girl stiffened, and looked around.

"You see," said Elinor, "my baby's fine."

In Zaddie's arms lay Frances Caskey, naked and limp, with Perdido river water dripping slowly from her elbows and feet.

"Come out of the water, Zaddie," said Elinor, drawing the girl out by the sleeve of her dress. "The bottom is muddy, and you could slide..."

Next morning, Roxie shook Zaddie out of her deep slumber, saying, "Child, you have not *begun* to rake this morning! What's wrong with you?" Zaddie dressed quickly, shaken but relieved that her previous night's adventure had been no more than a dream. She had wandered through a nightmare, reached safety, and been immediately overtaken with undisturbed sleep. It was unthinkable, in the light of morning, that Elinor would throw her newborn baby into the Perdido, and Zaddie didn't even allow herself to *think* of what she had caught in her arms in the dream.

She ran into the kitchen and gobbled a biscuit. Grabbing her rake from its accustomed corner, she flung open the back door. For a moment, the sound of those hinges brought back the dream; but Zaddie merely grinned at her own fear. She ran down the back steps—and stopped dead in her tracks.

There in the sand were four sets of footprints. Two

sets led down toward the river and two led back—
and around the returning set were tiny circular
depressions such as might be made where droplets
of water dripped into the sand and dried.

With a heavy heart, Zaddie stepped off into the
cool gray yard. With downcast eyes, she carefully
obliterated those sets of footprints leading to and
from the river, as if by that means she could blot out
what had not been, after all, a dream. All the while
she worked, she could hear Elinor on the second-floor
sleeping porch. She was crooning a little tuneless
song to her newborn baby.

CHAPTER 16

~~~~~~~~~~~~~~~~~~~~~~~~~~

Father, Son, and Holy Ghost

About the time of the birth of her niece Frances, Sister Caskey became overwhelmed with a sense of powerlessness and inconsequence. Why she should be so affected now, when before she had always taken her condition so much for granted, she did not know. Perhaps it had something to do with Oscar's marriage to Elinor, and his escaping the house while she remained behind, serving as a sponge to soak up Mary-Love's resentment at her son's desertion. Perhaps it was something about Elinor herself, who was younger than Sister, but unquestionably more powerful—Elinor had fought as an equal with Mary-Love. Perhaps Sister was tired of her mother's mingy complaints against Elinor, against the town, and against Sister herself. Recently, Mary-Love had made her first attempts to take a greater share of control over Miriam, whom she had always shared equally with her daughter. Sister thought she resented this most of all. She knew that soon Mary-Love would take the child away from her completely, and Sister would be alone again.

Although the Caskeys were better off than almost any other Perdido family, Sister had very little that was hers. She possessed no more than some odd stocks that had been birthday gifts and whose dividends were erratic and negligible. She remembered well enough the Caskey jewels, buried with Genevieve, which had so mysteriously appeared at the ceiling of the front bedroom of Elinor's house. But of that hoard, Sister had nothing at all. Except for the black pearls that Elinor took, Mary-Love had kept everything for herself and Miriam. Sister began to believe that her opinion was never solicited about any matter of consequence. One morning in July she showed up at James's office at the mill and declared herself fit and ready for any task that might be assigned to her. James looked at his niece in perplexity and misgiving, and said, "Lord, Sister, I cain't make heads or tails of this place myself, I don't know why you should be coming to *me* to tell you what you can do!" When she went to her brother with the same announcement, Oscar said, "Sister, there's nothing for you here, unless you can type-write or fix a broken-down chipper, and I know for a fact you cain't." Sister felt that the family was conspiring to keep her from the dignity and satisfaction of common human responsibilities.

She suggested to Mary-Love that she might open a store on Palafox Street to sell threads and buttons, but Mary-Love said, "No, Sister, I'm not gone give you the money, because the place would close down in six months. What do you know about running a shop? Besides, I want you here at home with me." When her mother said that, Sister realized that "at home" was exactly where she did not want to remain for the rest of her life.

Sister was weary of all of it, and Sister thought she saw a way out.

Her solution wasn't a new one; it was a remedy common all over the world. Procuring a husband would make all things right. As she began the task of looking about for likely candidates for the position, she discovered to her gratification that the most eligible man in Perdido—the one most exactly suited to her purposes—was also the handiest. He was the man whose snoring she heard at the other end of the hallway every night. Early Haskew.

Early was handsome, in a just-coming-in-out-of-the-sun sort of way. He was an engineer and looked to have a good future before him. All the Caskeys liked him. But none of this really mattered to Sister. What was most important about Early Haskew was that when the levee was finished, he would move away from Perdido. It was only to be assumed that if Early were married by that time, he would take his wife away with him.

Sister had no experience in even the simplest forms of flirtation and allurement, and in this matter she could scarcely go to her mother or her mother's friends for advice. Elinor was also out of the question. So Sister went where she had gone once or twice before, to Ivey Sapp, Mary-Love's cook and maid. She knew that Ivey's advice would be supernatural in its base—and in its execution—but she could see no alternative. So Sister, saying to herself, *I have nowhere else to turn,* went down into the kitchen one afternoon, and said to Ivey without preamble, "Ivey, you gone help me get married?"

"Sure will," said Ivey, without hesitation. "Somebody particular?"

Ivey Sapp had come to Mary-Love's house when

she was sixteen, about three years earlier. She was shiny black and plump. Her legs were permanently bowed from riding the Sapp mule round and round the cane crusher for sometimes twelve hours a day. Finally she had grown tired of the oppressive monotony of her existence at home, and longed for what her mother, Creola, contemptuously called "a life in the town." A kind of marriage had been arranged with Bray Sugarwhite, a man much older than Ivey, but he was kind and well situated in the Caskey household.

Ivey's principal fault—at least in Mary-Love's eyes—was a sort of rampant superstition that saw devils in every tree and portents in every cloud and dark meanings in every casual accident. Ivey Sapp slept with charms, and there were *things* on a chain around her neck. She wouldn't begin canning on a Friday, and would run off and not return for the rest of the day if she saw anyone open an umbrella in the house. She wouldn't carry out ashes after three o'clock in the afternoon lest there be a death in the family. She wouldn't sweep after dark because she'd sweep good fortune out the door. She wouldn't wash on New Year's day lest she wash a corpse in the ensuing year. She had many prohibitions and exceptions, and a little rhyme or saying for each, so that the days were scarce on which she performed without objection every task assigned her. Mary-Love sometimes said she believed that Ivey made up half of it in order to shirk her duties, but Ivey had plenty of superstition that was in no way connected with work. Thus it was a disconcerting fact of life in the Caskey household that the most innocent gesture observed by Ivey or unthinkingly reported to her elicited a dire prediction: "If you sing before you eat, you cry before you sleep," for instance. Before Miriam was born, Mary-Love always declared herself glad that there were no children in the house, because Ivey would have turned them into sniveling, frightened creatures, with her tales and warnings of things that waited for you in the forest and looked in your windows and hitched rides on the underside of your boat.

"So what am I supposed to do?" said Sister, having with some embarrassment confessed to Ivey that she wanted to marry none other than Early Haskew.

Ivey sat down at the kitchen table and appeared to lose herself in thought and incomprehensible murmurings as she began mechanically to snap the ends off a basinful of beans. Sister impatiently sat by, but dared not interrupt Ivey's reverie. Sister declared to herself that she put no faith in superstition or in Ivey's charms and rituals, but it was difficult to maintain that skepticism while Ivey sat before her in the midst of her incantatory monologue. After several minutes, Ivey's eyes fell closed; her hands dropped into her lap. She remained perfectly still for such a long time that Sister began to worry. Quite suddenly, Ivey's eyes snapped open, and she asked, "What's today?"

"Wednesday," replied Sister, quite as alarmed as if Ivey had said, *I have seen the Lord of the Evil Angels*.

"On Friday," said Ivey, "go out and buy me a live chicken."

Sister sat back, confused. "Ivey—"

"Don't buy it from a woman, make sure you buy it from a man. A chicken bought from a woman won't do us no good at all."

On Friday, Sister went downtown and loitered around Grady Henderson's store until Thelma Henderson left the counter to go into the back for something. Then Sister sprang out from behind a barrel, and cried, "Grady, can you get me a chicken, please? I'm in a real hurry."

"Thelma'll be right back out, Miz Caskey. She'll take care of you."

"Oh, Lord, Grady, I just looked at my watch"— she wasn't wearing one, and the grocer could see that too—"and I am supposed to have been back at the house half an hour ago. You know what Mama's gone say to me?"

Grady Henderson knew Mary-Love and could just about imagine. "Which one you want?" he asked, going over to the glass case where the chickens lay in porcelain trays.

"I need a live one, can you get me one out back? I got to have a spring chicken—that hasn't laid an egg yet," she added anxiously and with some embarrassment. "You've probably got one, haven't you?"

Grady Henderson looked at Sister closely, shrugged, and went out through a door in the rear. Sister followed him outside into a small dark shed that housed coops for fowl. "This one here," said Grady, pointing into a coop that contained half a dozen dirty white chickens of various sizes and ages.

Sister nodded. "She looks young." Mr. Henderson opened the coop, drew the chicken out by its neck and threw it into a scales that was hanging from the ceiling. "Two and a half pounds, that's about forty-five cents. Here, I'll put her in a bag and you go on inside and give Thelma the money."

"No," cried Sister in alarm, pulling a dollar bill from her pocket. "I'll just give this to you, Grady. You keep the change—I *got* to get on back home!"

"Miz Caskey, there is something wrong with you today. You gave me a whole dollar. Let me give you another chicken."

"No, I just want this one!" she cried. She drew

52

back her shoulders and, more quietly, assured him, "I'll be all right."

Then, holding out before her the croker sack with the chicken inside, Sister ran home, sneaking in the back way so her mother wouldn't see her.

"Your Mama's gone out," said Ivey, peering into the sack. "She say she be back for supper, so we gone do this thing right now."

"Don't we have to wait till it's dark?"

"What for? Who you been talking to, Miz Caskey? I know what I'm doing." Then, with no mystic passes or murmured incantations and with Sister still holding on to the sack, Ivey reached in and twisted off the head of the spring chicken. She pressed Sister's hands together and the top of the jerking sack closed. Sister held it at arm's length and watched with horror as spots of blood soaked through the burlap. When no motion could be detected, Ivey reached in and withdrew the body of the chicken. Its feathers were splattered with the blood that had poured out of its wrung neck. Holding the wretched fowl by the feet, Ivey slit open the breast of the chicken with a small knife, then pressed her pudgy fingers inside the carcass, groped around for a moment and then brought out its bloody heart. This she dropped unceremoniously onto a saucer on the kitchen table.

Leaving Sister to clean the kitchen of blood, Ivey buried the chicken and its head in a hole she had dug in the sand beside the kitchen steps. She folded the burlap and hid it beneath a stack of old newspapers on the back porch. Sister watched all this without daring to question what portion of this complex procedure was legitimate and necessary, and what part was only to keep the business secret from Mary-Love. Ivey motioned Sister to follow her back into the kitchen.

From a drawer of kitchen implements, Ivey took five skewers and laid them in a neat row on the kitchen table. She then seated herself before them, picked up the saucer that held the chicken's heart, and offered it to Sister. Sister gingerly plucked the heart off the plate.

Ivey smashed the saucer on the floor of the kitchen and motioned for Sister to walk around the table.

Sister, half-embarrassed, half-fearful, did so.

"Father, Son, and Holy Ghost," said Ivey.

"Father, Son, and Holy Ghost," repeated Sister. Following Ivey's silent directions, she paced around the table thrice, each time repeating that same incantation, the very familiarity of which was of comfort to Sister.

Sister ended her movement around the table standing beside Ivey's chair. The black woman then took up one of the skewers, handed it to Sister, and indicated a spot at the right side of the chicken heart that lay in Sister's outstretched hand. Sister had already understood that Ivey's directions were to be silent, except for the formulas, which Sister was to repeat *verbatim*. As Sister pierced the heart with the skewer and pressed it through, Ivey intoned, *"As I am piercing the heart of this innocent hen, so will Early Haskew's heart be thrust through with love of me."* Sister, with widened eyes, held the end of the skewer and repeated the words.

With the second skewer Ivey pointed a spot on the front of the chicken heart, and said, *"This thrust will pierce Early's heart until the day he asks me to be his wife."* Sister repeated these words as she pressed the skewer through.

The third skewer went from the back to the front, and Sister said, after Ivey, *"For life and for death, Early Haskew, I belong to you."*

The fourth skewer went from side to side, starting from the left. *"What's mine is yours, what's yours is mine."*

Ivey took up the last skewer and pressed a point

at the bottom of the heart. Sister pierced the heart from there, and the point of the skewer came out the top with a drop of blood on it. *"Five wounds had Jesus, and by them will you be stricken unto death, Early Haskew, if we are not man and wife within the year. In the name of the Father, and the Son, and the Holy Ghost. Amen."*

Sister was about to speak, protesting that she had no wish that the alternative to her marriage should be Early's death, but Ivey shook her head emphatically to enjoin silence. Ivey rose from the table, then went over to the stove and opened the grate. Sister noticed for the first time that Ivey had kept the stove hot all afternoon.

Sister tossed the skewered heart inside, where it fell upon a bed of glowing embers and began to sizzle. Sister and Ivey peered in and watched as it glowed red, and then burned with a crimson flame. Soon nothing was left but the five glowing skewers, which finally dropped down onto the coals, still interwoven into a pentagon.

Ivey slammed the stove door shut. The two women stood up straight, and in unison repeated the incantation that no longer seemed so familiar and comforting to Sister. *"In the name of the Father, the Son, and the Holy Ghost."*

CHAPTER 17

Dominoes

The first sawmill in Perdido had been built by Roland Caskey in 1875. The old man subsequently gained cutting control of eighteen thousand acres of timberland in Baldwin and Escambia counties. By 1895, when he died, the Caskey mill was producing twenty-five thousand feet of lumber a day. The cutdown trees that his Perdido mill couldn't handle were branded with a trefoil and sent down the Perdido to his backup mill at Seminole. Roland Caskey remained illiterate to his death, but he could look at a two-acre stand of timber and tell, within twenty board feet, how much lumber it would produce. He had had, moreover, the sense to marry a smart woman. Elvennia Caskey bore him two sons and a daughter. The daughter died, bitten by a water moccasin that one day slithered up the lawn out of the

Perdido, but the two sons grew up strong and fine. Because of their mother's efforts they were well-educated, well-mannered, and emotionally sensitive. Indeed, Roland complained of "the stamp of femininity" placed on his elder son James, which would render him soft and womanly.

When Roland Caskey had settled in the area, Baldwin and Escambia counties were wildernesses of pine, and it seemed inconceivable that the forests could ever be depleted, yet only three mills working at capacity began to accomplish this depletion. Expanding uses for resin and turpentine only made matters worse, for thousands of trees were "bled" by impoverished poachers. Once bled, a tree wasn't worth cutting. The forest retreated around Perdido and the barrens farther out grew less dense, as bled trees died and toppled in the first spring storm. Roland Caskey complained bitterly when the Secretary of the Interior proposed strict laws for the preservation of the forests and demanded rigid enforcement of earlier legislation.

Roland Caskey's will divided his holdings equally between his wife and his younger son Randolph, leaving only a small annual maintenance income to the other son James. He had dictated in the preamble of the document that he would not be able to sleep in his grave knowing that he had turned over the operation of his woodland empire to a man "with the stamp of femininity upon him." The day after the will was probated, however, Elvennia Caskey signed over her half to the disinherited son. But it was not for this generosity alone that James Caskey remained with his mother until her death, nursing her with unwavering filial affection through years of senility and physical helplessness. The idea of marriage never occurred to him without a concomitant sensation of having put something nasty into his mouth.

When James and Randolph, in concert rarely found among brothers, took over the operation of the Caskey mill, they began buying up all the land they could around Perdido. Their father and the other millowners had thought that the purchase of timberland was a wasteful expenditure of capital; it was much cheaper to pay landowners for the right to cut the timber. James and Randolph's policy was universally wondered at and ridiculed, but they persisted. Having bought the land, they systematically began to cut what was on it, and replanted immediately. Within five years the wisdom of their course was acknowledged and imitated by the Turks and the DeBordenaves. The old Puckett mill in Perdido was eventually forced out of business altogether, for there was no more standing timber for Mr. Puckett to buy.

The DeBordenave and Turk mills for twenty years ranked second and third to the Caskeys'. Sometimes the DeBordenaves had a better year than the Turks, and vice versa, but only the millowners themselves really knew which company was worth more. The Caskeys owned the most land, however, and had never ceased buying it up whenever the opportunity presented itself. Randolph Caskey died when his son Oscar was away at the University of Alabama. James ran the mill ineffectually for two years before Oscar returned to Perdido to accede to his father's place. Oscar and James, prodded by Mary-Love, would not hesitate to purchase two acres of slashpine surrounded by Turk forest. The smaller mills now worked the second and third growths of their land, but the Caskeys had some virgin forest, a rare thing in those parts.

Mary-Love and James Caskey owned the mill and the land, but Oscar ran the operation. James went to his office every day and occupied himself one way or another, principally in correspondence, but much

59

of that effort was dispensable; the work could have been done by a man hired at two thousand dollars a year. But the company could not have functioned without Oscar. For all his effort and long hours, though, he had no more money than poor old Sister, and as everybody knew, Sister had nothing at all.

People in town who didn't know anything about the family's situation looked at the three Caskey houses and drew their own conclusions from the fact that Elinor and Oscar lived in the biggest and the newest. Since it was also thought that without Oscar the mill would slip into insolvency within a few weeks, everyone naturally imagined that Oscar possessed a substantial portion of the Caskey treasure. That was not so. Oscar and Elinor didn't even own the house they lived in. It had been Mary-Love's gift, but Mary-Love had never put herself to the trouble of actually signing over the deed. Once when Elinor prodded Oscar to remind his mother of that omission, Mary-Love grew huffy and said, "Oscar, do you and Elinor imagine that you are in danger of being thrown out onto the street? Who do you think I am going to put in there instead of you? When you two were living right down the hall from me, and I didn't want you to leave *then,* do you think I am gone let you go farther away from me than right next door?" Oscar returned to Elinor and told her what his mother had said, but Elinor was not to be put off quite so easily. She sent Oscar back, and this time he got an even angrier reply from his mother: "Oscar, you and Elinor are gone *get* that house when I die! Do you want me to show you the *will?* Cain't you even wait till I am dead?" Oscar refused to broach the matter again, but Elinor was not satisfied.

Perdido residents would have been surprised at the modest size of Oscar's salary. Oscar once ventured to complain to James, who pleaded the case to his sister-in-law. Mary-Love said, "What do they need? Tell me, James, and I will go out and buy it. I will have Bray put it right on their front doorstep."

"Mary-Love, it's nothing like that," James replied. "They don't need new furniture or a new car or anything, but Elinor needs money to buy food every week. They need money to pay the coalman in winter. Oscar ordered a new set of ivory dominoes last week, and when they came in he had to borrow ten dollars from me to pay for 'em. Mary-Love, I say we give old Oscar a little bit more money. You know he earns it."

"You tell Oscar to come to me," said Mary-Love. "I will give my boy whatever he wants. You tell Elinor to knock on my front door. She will have her heart's desire."

Mary-Love liked to see herself as the family cornucopia, dispensing all manner of good things, unstintingly, unceasingly. She considered herself amply rewarded by her children's gratitude, and if she perceived that her children were not sufficiently grateful, she could make something of that, too. There was no difficulty in keeping Sister in a position of servile dependence, because, Mary-Love was certain, she had no prospect of marriage and no money of her own. Sister would never leave Perdido, her mother's house, or Mary-Love's fervid embrace. Oscar, though, had thrown himself into the bonds of matrimony with Elinor, and had thus weakened the emotional cords that had bound him to Mary-Love. The financial ties between mother and son, however, remained strong, or at least they would as long as Mary-Love had anything to say about it. Lady Bountiful had no intention of allowing Oscar to escape her boons.

Elinor understood all this and explained it to her husband.

Oscar replied, "You're probably right, Elinor.

That's probably how Mama does it. It makes me sorry for poor old Sister, too. But what am I gone do?"

"You can fight her. You can tell her you're going to leave that old mill high and dry if you don't get some decent money out of it. You can tell her that you and I are going to pack our bags and move to Bayou le Batre next Tuesday, and let her know that I'll be back in another month to pick up Miriam. That's what you can do."

"I cain't do that. Mama wouldn't believe me. Mama would call my bluff. What would you and I do in Bayou le Batre, that old place? I don't know anything about shrimp boats!"

"If James and your mama did right by you," Elinor went on, "they would give you a one-third interest in that mill. They would sign over to you one-third of all the Caskey land."

Oscar whistled at the very thought. "They won't do it, though."

"Maybe not right now," said Elinor thoughtfully, "but, Oscar, if you're not going to do anything, then it looks like it's going to be up to me..."

"What you thinking about doing?" Oscar asked uneasily.

"I don't know yet. But, Oscar, let me tell you something. There is no sacrifice I would not make to put you where you are supposed to be."

"Elinor, you shouldn't have to go out of your way for me. We get along pretty well, it seems to me."

"Not as well as we could, Oscar. I didn't marry just *any*body, you know. My daddy used to say he'd like to see the man *I'd* marry. My mama used to say he'd have to be mighty powerful or mighty rich."

Oscar laughed. "I guess you proved your mama and daddy wrong. I'm not powerful, and I'm certainly not rich."

"Mama and Daddy weren't wrong," said Elinor. Those words somehow didn't seem at home in Elinor's mouth; certainly she wasn't in the habit of speaking of her parents. "In fact, I have every intention of proving them right. Oscar, let me ask you something. What in the world would have been my purpose in coming to Perdido at all, if it wasn't to marry the best man in town?"

"You mean you married me because you thought I was rich and powerful?" He didn't seem in the least disturbed by the idea.

"Of course not. You know why I married you. But, Oscar, I have no intention of allowing you to continue to wear yourself out down at that mill just so James can buy crystal and silver and Miss Mary-Love can fill her safety-deposit box with diamonds while we are poor as poverty."

"Well, Elinor, you just tell me what to do, and I'll do it. I wouldn't mind having a lot of money."

"Good," replied his wife. "So when I tell you to jump, you'll jump?"

"Right over the roof!"

Recently, a mania for the game of dominoes had infected the male population of Georgia, Alabama, and Florida. Perdido had not been immune. The malady took hold with virulence, and in the first hectic flush of fever there had been domino parties every night throughout the town. Now that first unhealthy spasm had subsided, but many men continued to play regularly. Among these were the men of the 3 mill families, James Caskey, Oscar Caskey, Tom DeBordenave, and Henry Turk.

Every Monday and Wednesday evening at six-thirty they gathered at the square red table in Elinor's breakfast room, joined by three others: Leo Benquith, Warren Moye, and Vernell Smith. Leo Benquith was the most respected doctor in town. Warren Moye was a dapper little man who stood behind the desk of the Osceola Hotel every day; he always brought with him a cushion, which he transferred from chair to chair to ease the pain of his everlasting hemorrhoids. Vernell Smith was rather in the character of a dwarf jester at the Spanish court; he was young and desperately ugly, with a long face that reminded farm folks of the head of a stillborn calf, except that Vernell's had a number of large moles with long hairs in them.

On Mondays and Wednesdays, Elinor took special care to keep the doors to the breakfast room closed all evening long, for every one of those men smoked cigars or cigarettes and the smoke could fill the house. Every Monday and Wednesday afternoon Zaddie took down the curtains in that room so that they would not become impregnated with the odor of tobacco. During the game, the countless cigar and cigarette butts were thrown into a glass cistern of water the size of a fishbowl. After a couple of hours, the room was always so filled with smoke that Zaddie could not come in to empty the cistern without her eyes immediately watering. And the room was noisy. The men growled and slammed their ivory dominoes down on the square table. The shuffling was thunderous and could be heard all over the house. There was no cursing, except an occasional "damn." With the exception of Vernell Smith, all these men went to Sunday school. The stories and the tales traded over that red table in the course of the evening were not so different from the stories and tales that Perdido ladies told over their afternoon bridge games.

On these evenings, Elinor and Zaddie sat on the front porch or on the porch upstairs. Elinor sewed and Zaddie read. Soon it became the custom for one of the other domino wives to come over with her husband and spend the evening with Elinor or to call and talk to her on the telephone. Whenever the visitor was Manda Turk or Caroline DeBordenave, Elinor showed an uncommon and insatiable interest

in the details of their husbands' mills, soaking up
every detail of the lumber business that those two
women could summon up from minds untrained to
such matters. Manda and Caroline agreed that Elinor must have a motive for the acquisition of this
information, though Elinor declared that it was only
curiosity. When the domino party finally broke up,
the domino wife had already gone home alone and
Elinor and Zaddie had gone to bed.

As Oscar saw his friends out the front door and
the men spoke their good-nights, each one—except
modest James Caskey—would relieve himself against
one of Elinor's newly planted camellias. Then Oscar
would wander back into the house and call out
loudly, "Zaddie, get up and lock the doors!" Oscar
was a kind man and a good one, but he had been
trained to laziness by his mother, and if there was
anything he could get a woman to do for him, he
wouldn't hesitate to ask her to do it. As Oscar
trudged upstairs, Zaddie would open the windows of
the breakfast room, pour the cistern of butts out into
the sandy yard, lock the front door, turn out all the
lights, return to her own closet, and with eyes still
smarting from the smoke, lie down upon her cot and
drift into sleep.

One Monday evening, while the men played downstairs, Elinor Caskey and Caroline DeBordenave sat
on the porch upstairs. Frances's crib had been
brought out and placed so that as the two women
rocked in the swing they could peer over at the child.
Elinor as usual had brought up the subject of the
lumber business, and Caroline—knowing her host-
ess's interest in the topic by this time—had come
prepared with information. She had questioned her
husband to some extent at supper, and though he
was surprised by his wife's sudden interest in what

had never seemed to matter to her before, he answered all her questions in detail.

"No, Elinor," said Caroline shaking her head, "it's just not going well for Tom. Now, I'm sure I'm not telling you anything new, because Tom said that both Henry Turk and Oscar knew about his trouble. It's strange, Tom never told *me*. I was so surprised! The flood did it. Tom lost all his records. He says he remembers that he had almost a hundred thousand dollars..." Caroline paused, unable to remember the precise term her husband had employed.

"In uncollected bills?" suggested Elinor.

"That's right," said Caroline complacently. Her tone suggested that she was gossiping about some small matter that was of no possible consequence to her, and indeed it seemed to Caroline as if it were not. The mills were matters for men. She assumed that nothing could or ever would interfere with the money Tom gave her every month to run the household and buy clothes; with her needs taken care of, Tom could do what he pleased with all the rest. "See, Elinor, the problem is, he not only lost all *that* money, but he lost all the lumber that was stored at the mill *and* all the lumber that he took out to Mr. Madsen's place, because Mr. Madsen's barn washed away too. Then most of the machinery got filled with mud and that had to be replaced, and now there's no money. Tom says he doesn't know how he's going to be able to go on."

"Can't he borrow?" asked Elinor.

"Well, not much," said Caroline, with a little pride that she had taken care to ask her husband this question. "He went to the bank in Mobile and went down on twenty knees in front of the president asking for money to build the mill back up, but the president of the bank said, 'Mr. DeBordenave, how do we know there's not gone be another flood?'"

"Because there's not!" said Elinor, definitely.

66

"Well, I certainly hope not," returned Caroline. "Even my best rugs had to be just thrown out. I was never so unhappy in all my life. Anyway, Tom said the bank wouldn't lend him any money because they thought that another flood was gone come along and wash everything away a second time."

"So he can't get the money?"

"Well, maybe he can and maybe he cain't. The banks say that they *will* lend money after the levee's built, but not before. So Tom is real anxious to get that thing put up. He just hopes he can hold out long enough. I hope he can, too," Caroline concluded reflectively. "When Tom is worried about that old mill, he doesn't pay one bit of attention to anything else in the world."

After Caroline had gone home, Elinor remained on the porch with Frances, and, against her custom, waited up for Oscar. When he came up the stairs she called him out onto the porch and said, "Oscar, Caroline was telling me Tom is having trouble borrowing from the banks."

"Well, yes," replied Oscar hesitantly. "Fact is, we all are. Nobody's gone lend us any money to build up again until the levee goes up."

"What would happen if the levee *never* got built?"

Oscar sat down beside his wife. "Are you really interested?"

"Of course I am!"

"Well," said Oscar, sitting back and folding his hands behind his head, rocking the swing lightly, "old Tom would fold up his tents, I guess."

"What about us?"

"Well, we'd go along all right for a while. We'd get by, I guess."

"Just get by?"

"Elinor, what we're trying to do right now is build back up what we lost in the flood. But then if we really want to get the place going, then we've got to expand. We cain't do that without borrowing the money. There's not a bank in this state—or out of it for that matter—who's gone lend us money till the levee's built. *That's* why we're working so hard on this business. You see now?" Elinor nodded slowly. "I am dead on my feet," said Oscar. "You want to come to bed?"

"No," said Elinor, "I'm not tired yet. You go on."

Oscar rose, leaned down over the crib to kiss sleeping Frances, and went inside the house.

Long after Oscar had undressed, knelt at the side of his bed to pray, lain himself down and fallen as deeply asleep as his daughter, Elinor remained awake. She sat in the swing, rocking slowly and staring out into the darkness. In the black night, the water oaks swayed in the slightest wind. A few rotted branches, covered with a dry green fungus, dropped twigs and leaves, or sometimes fell whole, with a crack and a thump, on the sandy ground. Beyond, the Perdido flowed, muddy and black and gurgling, carrying dead things and struggling live ones inexorably toward the vortex in the center of the junction.

CHAPTER 18

Summer

Summer came to Perdido. Elinor continued to ponder about her husband's minuscule salary and the Caskeys' substantial wealth. Sister pushed open the back door every morning to stare at the barely discernible mound beneath which the eviscerated chicken lay buried and wondered when Early Haskew was going to propose, or, conversely, when he was going to die. James Caskey sighed and looked about and counted off his loneliness on his ten fingers—it seemed as substantial as that! Mary-Love greedily watched the engineer's daily progress on the plans for the levee, anticipating with great satisfaction the effect the construction would have on her daughter-in-law. And every morning Zaddie's patient rake still made patterns in the sandy yards around the three Caskey houses.

Only children really loved the summer, for of course there was no school. The days were long, unbroken by hours and tasks and bells. It was odd, to Grace Caskey, how each summer was different and possessed its own character. Last summer she had played with the Moye children constantly, and now this summer she saw them only once a week at Sunday school. Every day the previous summer, Bray had driven her out to Lake Pinchona, where a swimming pool with concrete sides was fed by the biggest artesian well in the entire state. A monkey in a wire cage nipped at her fingers when she stuck them through the mesh. This summer she hadn't been out there once, even though they had begun to build a dance hall on stilts out over the muddy, shallow lake. The owners had imported alligators from the Everglades to stock Lake Pinchona, both for picturesque effect and in order to discourage bathers from swimming anyplace other than the easily policed concrete pool.

This summer of 1922 was given over to Zaddie Sapp. Grace was entranced by Zaddie. Grace worshipped the thirteen-year-old black girl and everything about her. Grace followed Zaddie around all day, and would scarcely let the black girl out of her sight. In the morning, she would help Zaddie rake in those portions of the yard invisible to Mary-Love's windows; Mary-Love didn't approve of Grace's helping servants. When Zaddie had finished work, Grace would go over to Elinor's house and Roxie, on temporary loan from James, would fix them dinner. Grace thought it a huge privilege to be allowed to eat in the kitchen with Roxie and Zaddie, and scorned a place at the dining room table with Elinor and Oscar. After dinner, Oscar gave each of the girls a quarter and told them to go down to the Ben Franklin and pick out whatever they wanted. The girls walked downtown hand in hand and roamed the aisles of the dime store. They pointed at everything and looked at everything with such intensity that they grew more familiar with the stock than the man who owned the store. Each purchased three small items with that quarter and tumbled them together in one sack. At home they took out their purchases and examined them minutely. Trading them back and forth, they wrapped the best one in colored paper and presented it to the other, and finally laid them all away with another hundred similar fragile happinesses in a hinged wooden box on the back porch of Elinor's house.

This unscreened porch, which was long and high-ceilinged and always shadowy and cool even in the hottest weather, was called the lattice, because of its crisscrossed woodwork. Like the rest of the house, it was raised high above the level of the yard outside, so that the infrequent breezes blew beneath it and through it. One of the windows of Zaddie's tiny room opened onto this lattice. The children could crawl in and out, with the aid of Zaddie's cot on one side and an old broken chair on the other.

On this cool lattice Zaddie and Grace invented, perfected, and played a hundred different games, the complex rules of which pertained only to themselves and to the geography and furnishings of the lattice itself. Grace took so many meals there and spent so much time with Zaddie, that Mary-Love began to complain to James that Grace had moved in to Elinor's, was bothering Elinor, and was always waking up Frances. How she could know this, when there was virtually no communication between the households, Mary-Love did not explain. James simply said, "Grace is still lonely with her mama dead, and I am not about to interfere in anything that makes her happy."

That her niece should find such profound pleasure in the company of a thirteen-year-old black girl—

and, more to the point, always within the precincts of Elinor's house—was a slap in Mary-Love's face. She decided, without saying anything more to James, to wreck Grace's perfection of happiness. Grace would learn that she, Mary-Love, was the source of all felicity within the Caskey family.

Tom and Caroline DeBordenave had two children. The elder was a girl, fifteen, pretty, popular, and smart. Her name was Elizabeth Ann. The boy, four years younger, was called John Robert, and he was a problem. John Robert was thought fortunate to have been born into a family who would always be able to take care of him, for it was obvious he would never be able to take care of himself. He was a sweet, quiet child, but simple. In school, he was three grades behind, which is to say that he generally spent two years in any one grade, and even so he was always far behind his classmates. Promotions were granted not because he deserved them, but because it would have been cruel to keep him back longer. He sat at the back of the room, and was allowed to draw on tablets throughout the school day, no matter what the rest of the class did. He wasn't called on to answer questions or to read aloud, and when the others took tests, John Robert turned over the page of his tablet, bent down over it, and pretended that he too was in the way of being examined. At recess, John Robert didn't play organized games with the boys because he never quite managed to get the rules straight in his clouded mind, and he hadn't the coordination to jump rope with the girls. Every morning, however, Caroline DeBordenave filled his pockets with candy, and for a few minutes at the beginning of morning recess John Robert was very popular. Boys and girls surrounded him, tickled him, called out his name, and rifled his pockets until there was not a single piece of candy left. Then all the children went away to their games, and John Robert sat sighing on the bench next to his teacher, or on favored days, beat erasers against the side of the building until he and the bricks were white with chalk dust.

In school John Robert was happy, for if he didn't participate in the activities of his bustling schoolmates, the crackling industry of study and play surrounded him constantly. If he might sometimes be lonely, he was never alone. In the summers, however, no one thought of him. His mother still filled his pockets with candy, but that weight dragged on him through the day. By suppertime, the chocolate and the peppermint had melted into one sticky and unappetizing mass. Elizabeth Ann sometimes read to him. She rocked in a chair on the front porch, while he stood beside her with his elbow on the arm so that one whole side of his body moved up and down with the motion. Elizabeth Ann's voice was comfortingly near, but the meaning of the words she read was far away from John Robert.

He was lonelier this summer than ever before. Elizabeth Ann had been given a bicycle for Christmas and every day rode out to Lake Pinchona and took lessons in diving from a boy who was old enough to join the army. She also fed the monkey, and sometimes leaned out the windows of the dance hall and dropped hunks of stale bread down among the blooming water lilies below, hoping to attract the notice of the alligator that swam lazily among the pilings.

But John Robert wasn't permitted to ride a bicycle for fear he would be run down, and he wasn't allowed to go to Lake Pinchona for fear he would fall into the swimming pool and drown or lean too far out the dance hall window and drop down among the lily pads, where the alligator waited for choicer morsels than Elizabeth Ann's stale bread. So John Robert sat on the front steps of his house blinking at the sun, with his pockets filled with melting candy, forever in disappointed expectation of some child running up, calling his name, tickling his ribs, and rifling his pockets.

One day Mary-Love Caskey telephoned Caroline DeBordenave and said, "Caroline, your little boy is lonely. I see him sitting for hours and hours on your front steps, lonesome as an old country graveyard. I am gone send James's Grace over there and keep that child company."

"I wish you would," sighed Caroline. "John Robert doesn't know what to do without school. The summer takes the heart right out of John Robert. Some people are just sensitive to heat, I suppose." Caroline DeBordenave's way of dealing with John Robert's mental infirmity was not to deal with it at all, outwardly. She would attribute his silence, his vacancy, his manifold incapacities to anything but an incurably feeble intellect. But even if she always seemed to deny her son's handicaps, there was a reason that she filled his pockets with candy every day.

So the next morning, just as Grace and Zaddie were beginning their day's elaborate games on Elinor's lattice, the telephone rang in the house, and Elinor appeared a minute later and said, "Grace, Miss Mary-Love wants you over at her house right away."

And Grace went—in a sort of perplexed daze, for it wasn't easy to remember the last time she had been so summoned. Mary-Love sat in the front parlor, and of all surprising things to see on the sofa beside her, there sat John Robert DeBordenave in a new yellow playsuit with half a dozen sticks of peppermint candy protruding from the breast pocket.

"Grace," said Mary-Love, "here is John Robert who I have invited over here to play with you."

"Ma'am?"

"You and John Robert are gone have a good time for the whole summer, I know it."

74

Grace looked with some misgiving at John Robert, who was smiling timidly and alternately picking first at a button and then at a scab on his knee, about to dislodge both.

"You don't seem to have the little friends around this summer that you had last summer, Grace, and when I mentioned that to Caroline DeBordenave, she said to me, 'Goodness gracious! John Robert is all alone, too.' So Caroline and I have decided that you and John Robert are gone spend the rest of your summer together. You will have such fun!"

Grace began to understand. "I *have* friends," she protested. "I have Zaddie!"

"Zaddie is a little colored girl," Mary-Love pointed out. "It's all right to play with Zaddie, but she's not your real friend. John Robert can be your *real* little friend."

Grace thought she began to detect some small piece of injustice here, but before she could put her finger upon what it was exactly, Mary-Love went on: "Now I want you two to go and start playing together. I'll send Ivey to get you when it's time to eat. You and John Robert are gone have dinner with me every day."

It wasn't that Grace disliked John Robert. She felt sorry for him, and always in school went out of her way to be nice to him, always asking permission before she ransacked his pockets for candy. He was a boy, though, and his mind wasn't right. She would never love John Robert DeBordenave the way that she loved Zaddie Sapp.

"All right, Aunt Mary-Love," said Grace slyly, "I'll take John Robert over to Elinor's and we'll play on the lattice."

"No, you won't," said Mary-Love. "You can play in this house or you can play in John Robert's house. You cain't play in Elinor's house because I don't want you bothering Elinor and I don't want you bothering Elinor's baby."

"Well, can we play in *my* house?"

"May we play," corrected Mary-Love. "No, you may not. There is nobody to watch you over there."

"I don't *need* to be watched!"

Mary-Love sat silent and glanced at John Robert. Grace understood perfectly well what that silence and that glance meant, but she refused to be drawn into her aunt's conspiracy.

"All right, ma'am" said Grace sullenly, "but I got to go tell Zaddie I'm not coming back this morning."

"No, you don't," said Mary-Love. "There is no reason for you to explain yourself to a little colored girl who is hired to do something else besides play on a lattice porch all summer long. So, John Robert, what do you think you and Grace would like to do *this* morning?"

John Robert looked about the parlor astonished, realizing for the first time—and still dimly—that the new playsuit, this enforced visit, Grace's presence, and the conversation between her and Miss Mary-Love, all had something to do with him.

Mary-Love could have broken up Zaddie and Grace's friendship that summer if she had mounted a campaign of eternal vigilance, but she hadn't the time or the inclination for such warfare. She chose, rather, to imagine that she had crushed the enemy in a single blow, but Mary-Love did not take into account the depth of Grace's attachment to Zaddie. Grace found ways around Mary-Love's prohibition against having anything to do with the black girl, and ways to make the eternal presence of John Robert DeBordenave less onerous.

First, Grace went to Elinor and told her what had happened. Elinor said nothing at first, but by the expression on her face, her sympathies clearly lay with Grace and Zaddie. "You can come over here as much as you want this summer, Grace," said Elinor. "And you bring the DeBordenave boy over here too. Though I must say that I think it is a mistake for Caroline DeBordenave to give a ten-year-old girl charge of her child, who is *not* right in the head."

So Grace's afternoons with Zaddie continued, but they were no longer perfect, because of the presence of John Robert DeBordenave. Previously both girls had been good to John Robert, and on several occasions Zaddie had been called over to the De-Bordenaves' to watch him on Monday afternoons when Caroline was at bridge. Now, however, the two girls grew to resent John Robert because his company was forced upon them every day—and for so many hours. His conversational ability was limited almost entirely to pantomimic actions and an occasional word, which he always had to repeat at least three times before he could be understood. And he hadn't the remotest notion of what Zaddie and Grace's complex games were all about, but would blunderingly attempt to join in all the same. From resentment, there was only a short step to cruelty.

Grace began to taunt the boy. John Robert didn't exactly understand taunts, but he could sense the contempt behind them. Grace would take candy from his pockets, shove it into his mouth, and force him to swallow it whole. She deliberately spilled milk and iced tea on his new clothes, and then cried, "You are so clumsy, John Robert DeBordenave!" If he broke any of her Ben Franklin treasures—as he tended to do if he so much as picked one up—Grace would snatch the pieces away from him and then fling them in his face. She would never say, It's all right, you couldn't help it, when he began to weep large silent tears. Grace ignored the infirmity that crippled the child and saw only his exasperating slowness. She took note only of his inhibiting presence, and thought of him only as the instrument by which Mary-Love sought to separate her and Zaddie. If Grace was ashamed of her cruelties at all, she laid the blame at Mary-Love's door.

One day when John Robert was standing in the open door of the lattice staring out at the Perdido, Grace, without a thought to the consequences, ran up from behind, and shoved him down the steps.

He tumbled over and over, banging his head on the sharp corner of the bottom step. When Grace ran down and lifted his head, blood dripped from the wound and filled a groove in the patterned sand below.

Elinor, alerted to the accident by Grace's hysterical screams, called Dr. Benquith. John Robert was brought back to consciousness, examined, bandaged, and carried home by Bray. Grace ran along behind Bray, explaining tearfully, "He fell. He fell down the back steps and rolled all the way to the bottom!"

Grace was certain everyone knew that she had pushed John Robert. But her aunt said only, "How could you have let it happen? Why weren't you watching? You know that boy doesn't have sense enough to come in out of the rain!"

At first, Grace was relieved that her culpability had not been found out; it was better to be charged merely with neglect of duty than with murder. But as the days passed, Grace came to see that, because she had not been charged with the crime, she must bear all the guilt within herself. She was morose and downcast; her appetite was gone and her sleep was racked with nightmares. James worried about her. Mary-Love said, "She *ought* to feel guilty—that boy could have died! How would she have felt then? How would *we* have felt?"

Elinor called Grace to her one afternoon. Elinor sat in a swing on the upstairs porch, stood Grace before her, and said, "You feel real bad about John Robert, don't you?"

Grace nodded slowly. "Yes, ma'am. Is he gone die?"

"Of course not! Who told you that?"

"Aunt Mary-Love said he might. She said it would be my fault if he did!"

Elinor bit her lip for a moment, glanced over Grace's shoulder at Mary-Love's house, and then said, "John Robert is not going to die, and even if he did, it still wouldn't be your fault. You understand me, Grace?"

Grace trembled and bit *her* lip, then suddenly burst into tears and plunged her head into Elinor's lap. "It would be, it would be!" wailed Grace. "I pushed him!"

"Oh..." said Elinor slowly. "I see..."

Without removing Grace's head from her lap, Elinor moved the child around and drew her up into the swing beside her. Grace cried for a few minutes more, then sat up, red-eyed.

"All right, tell me what happened," said Elinor, and Grace told her.

"And you don't know why you did it?" Elinor asked when Grace had finished her description of the event.

"No, ma'am, 'cause I like old John Robert. I just didn't like having to take care of him all the time. Sometimes Zaddie and I just wanted to be by ourselves!"

Grace sat beside Elinor a long while, now feeling a great deal better for her confession. When at last Elinor drew apart and stood up, she said, "Grace, I'm going to speak to Caroline DeBordenave for a few minutes."

"You gone tell her I pushed John Robert?" cried Grace in a frenzy of terror and guilt.

"No," said Elinor. "I'm going to tell her that it was *not* your fault that John Robert fell down the back

79

steps, that we were all sorry it happened, but that you had no business being a nursemaid for John Robert for the entire summer. You are too young to have that kind of responsibility. If she had wanted John Robert watched every minute of the day, then she should have hired a colored girl to do it. That's what I will say, and I will tell her how bad you feel—even though it *wasn't* your fault—and that you want permission to go visit John Robert and ask him how he's feeling. You do, don't you?"

"Yes, ma'am!" cried Grace vehemently, and meant it.

Caroline DeBordenave understood all that Elinor said, and agreed with her. "Lord, Elinor, when Bray brought John Robert home and I saw all that blood I was just about out of my mind! I didn't mean to slam the door in poor old Grace's face, it's just that I wasn't thinking straight. John Robert means more to Tom and me than anything else in the world. If anything happened to that boy, I don't know what we'd do. I suppose we would pack up and move away. I don't think either one of us would have the heart to stay behind."

Grace and Zaddie were no longer forced to bear the company and responsibility of John Robert DeBordenave. Mary-Love's scheme, undermined by Elinor's interference, came to nothing.

CHAPTER 19

The Heart, the Words, the Steel, and the Smoke

Sister wondered, that summer, how she could have been so foolish as to allow Ivey Sapp to cast a spell upon her and upon Early Haskew. Sister remembered with shuddering embarrassment how she had walked around the kitchen table with a bleeding chicken heart in her hand, and how she had spoken words over it, how she had skewered it, how she had thrown it into the fire. She prayed no one ever found out how silly she had been. Now, when she brought that scene to mind, her recollection involuntarily saw a row of human heads in the window of the kitchen; the heads had eyes that watched her movements, ears that heard her words, and mouths that would spread the humiliating story all over town.

Yet nothing happened. Even her most suspicious inquiry could detect no knowledge of the business in the faces that passed her on the street or in the voices that greeted her each day. The mound beside the back steps, beneath which the remains of the sacrificed chicken were buried, had been beaten down by the rain and one could no longer tell where it had been.

If Sister felt relief that her foolishness had not been discovered, she was also chagrined to find that the spell so far hadn't seemed to have had any effect. When she was alone in the house with Early, Sister sat in a good dress on the best sofa in the usually closed front parlor, conspicuously ready to accept a proposal of marriage. Early would only pass by and say, "Good Lord, Sister, aren't you burning up in there?"

Sister would sigh, get up from the sofa, and close the parlor doors, then go upstairs and change into something that was less appropriate for a proposal, but more comfortable for the weather. She decided, after several repetitions of this, that a man as straightforward as Early Haskew wasn't to be caught only by spells and stratagems. Sister realized she could not just simply put herself in the way of being asked; she would have to press the matter. If she hadn't much experience in dealing with men, well then, Early Haskew—who had always lived with *his* mother—probably hadn't had much opportunity to deal with young women. She doubted whether he had ever proposed to anyone, and if he had not, why should she assume that he would recognize, when she displayed it, the proper attitude of availability?

Thereafter, whenever Early was in his sitting room working on the plans for the levee Sister loitered there, and made no attempt to cover the fact that she *was* loitering. If Early went out to inspect a riverbank or talk to someone whose shed would be moved or examine a vein of clay out in the forest, Sister begged permission to come along with him.

"It's just gone be boring, Sister!" he'd exclaim.

Sister would reply, without a trace of a simper, "Lord, Early, I just like being with you!"

This tactic began to work. Soon she didn't bother to ask. When she saw him going out the door and climbing into the automobile, she would hop right into the back seat and say, "Where we going today? Who we gone speak to, Early?"

If it happened that Sister was in another part of the house and didn't see him go out the door, Early would linger in front of the car, and when Sister appeared at a window he would call out: "Hey, Sister, you holding me up!"

"You are bothering Early, Sister," said Mary-Love every evening at the supper table, quite as if Early were not sitting at her right hand.

"If Early doesn't want me trailing along behind him," said Sister, "then Early ought to tell me to stay at home."

"Sister's good help to me, Miz Caskey."

"How? How? I'd like to know."

"Well, she writes down my figures for me. She carries along a little notebook, and that frees me up. And she knows the people, too. Sister, I bet you know everybody in this town! We get over there in Baptist Bottom, I'm gone need some help. The way those colored people speak, hard sometimes for me to understand what they're talking about—in Pine Cone, colored people speak totally different—and I need Sister there to tell me what they've been saying to me."

"Sister is a drag on your work, Early," said Mary-Love, who had begun to see what was happening, and had set about to head it off before anything serious came of it.

83

So every evening Mary-Love objected to how much trouble Sister was for Early, and always dismissed his protestations to the contrary as mere politeness. And every evening she demanded that Sister leave the man alone for thirty minutes at least, but Sister merely shrugged and said, "Mama, I'm doing what I want to do because I'm happy doing it. So don't expect me to leave off just because it's what you want." Mary-Love thought about asking Early to leave the house altogether, but for several reasons she couldn't bring herself to do so. For one thing she had begged him to come, and the whole town knew it and he had probably even kept the two letters that she had written to him so she couldn't ask him to leave now without risking a severe ebbing of her reputation. He also remained a goad in the side of Elinor Caskey next door, and Mary-Love wouldn't have removed that goad for the world. At last she decided to give up any further subversion, trusting that Sister's bumbling inexperience would soon sink this matter-of-fact romance. Still, Mary-Love had nagging worries that some kind of attachment might be growing between her daughter and the engineer.

And indeed the day soon came that Mary-Love had feared and Sister had hoped for—when Sister was proven to be right and Mary-Love was shown to be wrong.

It was a particularly hot day in August. Sister and Early had driven far out into the country, over toward Dixie Landing on the Alabama River to a clay quarry that was of interest to Early. He and Sister had left Bray with the automobile at the single store at Dixie Landing. With sandwiches and a bottle of milk in a basket, they set out along a faint track in the pine forest. They found the quarry, and as Sister sat on a tolerably clean outcropping of sandstone Early climbed all about the pit, getting himself quite red and dusty in the process. "It won't do," was his judgment.

After this inspection, instead of returning directly to the car, they climbed over the lip of the quarry and went down the other side to Brickyard Lake. This was a wide shallow depression of blue water in a vast green pasture in sight of the wide gray Alabama River. In contrast to the river they saw before them, and in contrast to the rivers that wound through Perdido, the water of Brickyard Lake was extraordinarily blue and beautiful. There was a solitary clump of cypress on the near margin of the lake, and as Sister and Early made their way down to it, intending to picnic in its shade, they discovered first that the ground was too soggy to allow pleasant picnicking, and second that there was a little boat, with two oars inside, tethered to a tree. As was the custom in that part of Alabama, they requisitioned the craft for their own pleasure.

"I made cookies, too," said Sister, as she climbed into the boat.

Early rowed out toward the center of the lake. A kingfisher screeched in the branches of the cypress, and then swooped down into the water not twenty feet from them.

"Do I snore?" asked Early suddenly, after they had glided along several minutes in silence.

"You sure do," replied Sister energetically.

"Mama used to say I did. Does it keep you awake, though?"

"Sometimes," said Sister. "But I don't mind. I can always take a nap if I'm tired in the afternoon."

"You're at the other end of the hall."

"Yes," said Sister, unwrapping a sandwich for him and reaching forward with it. "But, Early, once you get going, you are pretty loud."

He set the oars behind him and took the sandwich.

He ate it so quickly that he was finished before Sister had even taken the first bite out of hers.

"I was starved."

"You should have said something. We didn't have to wait."

"But what if you were in the same room?"

Sister's mouth was full. She cocked her head, to indicate *What?*

"If we were in the same room," said Early, "you wouldn't be able to sleep at all because of my snoring." He seemed troubled by this thought.

Sister continued to eat her sandwich.

"So you wouldn't, would you?" asked Early, casting down his eyes.

"Wouldn't what?"

"Wouldn't want to get married?"

Sister gobbled up the last of her sandwich. "Early Haskew, is that what you have been going on about?"

"Yes, what'd you think?"

"I couldn't begin to imagine. Who cares if you snore? Daddy used to snore all the time. And he's been dead twenty years. What I mean is, it obviously didn't hurt Mama any, since she's outlived him that long."

"So you will think about marrying me? Sister, you got another sandwich?" Pleasure and happy expectation appeared to increase Early's appetite.

Sister reached in her basket and brought out another. "On one condition," she said.

"What's that?"

"That we don't live with Mama."

"Is that why you would say yes to marrying me, to get away from Miss Mary-Love? Miss Mary-Love has been very good to me."

"Miss Mary-Love is not your mama. Early, I am gone marry you because I am in *love* with you, and for no other reason in the world. Except that it would give me a good deal of satisfaction to leave Mama high and dry."

Early Haskew put the oars of the boat back in the water and rowed around the edge of Brickyard Lake three times. He would have done it again but Sister reminded him that Bray was probably starting to get nervous.

In the course of the walk from the lake back to Dixie Landing, Sister smiled a secret smile of pride that she had engineered the engagement herself, without the help of Ivey and Ivey's spell-casting. She regretted that she had ever so much doubted her own power as to have gone to Ivey in the first place.

Then her smile of pride faded. Sister saw that, after a manner, the spell *had* worked. Ivey had sacrificed a chicken and torn out its heart. Sister had spoken words over that heart, pierced it five times with steel, and had inhaled the smoke of its burning. Now she was engaged to Early Haskew. There was no way that she could bestow all the credit on herself.

It could have been the heart of that hen — and the steel and the words and the burning smoke—that accomplished the deed.

How could she ever know for certain?

CHAPTER 20

Queenie

Early intended to tell Mary-Love Caskey that very evening of his engagement to her daughter, but Sister cautioned against this course. "Mama's gone make trouble, or at least she's gone try."

"Why?" asked Early simply. "I thought your mama liked me."

"Of course she does. But not in the person of a son-in-law. Mama wouldn't approve of my intended if he was the King of the Jews dropped down on the front steps with a shoebox full of diamonds. Mama is not gone want to let me go, that's all."

"Sister, I don't mind trouble. I can stand up to your mama."

They were still making their way through the woods from Brickyard Lake toward the Landing, where Bray waited with the automobile. They had spent hours on the water in their borrowed boat and now the sun was in its decline. The woods were shadowed, but the sunlight now and then broke through the tops of the trees and blinded them for a moment as they walked along hand in hand.

"Of course you can, Early. That's not the point. I'm thinking about the levee."

"How you mean?"

"I mean, I think you ought to finish off all your plans and get everything set before we tell Mama anything. 'Cause there's bound to be trouble, and if there's trouble, then you won't get your work done like you should. Besides, you couldn't rightly go away on a honeymoon with me if you hadn't finished what you had set out to do, could you?"

"I could not," said Early stoutly, proud that his fiancée should see the thing in so responsible, practical, and—when it came down to it—so *masculine* a perspective.

For a time nothing was said. Sister told Ivey of the engagement. To Sister's relief Ivey said only, "I'm so happy for you, Sister!" and made no mention of the buried chicken. Everything continued as before, except that Sister, having reached her goal, spent less time with Early. Mary-Love grew complacent, and imagined a cooling between the two. Sister, she thought, had at last been discouraged by Early's inattentiveness to her.

Early was working harder, knowing that when he had completed the plans he would have not only the cash bonus promised by James Caskey, but Sister's hand in marriage. From the back pages of a periodical he purchased at the pharmacy he cut out an advertisement and sent away for a patented guaranteed cure for snoring. Every day he expectantly awaited its arrival. He once had heard his mother say that she had almost abandoned his father on account of his nocturnal wheezings and snufflings, and he had no wish to take any such chances with Sister when they should share the same bed.

Summer gradually and grudgingly gave way to autumn. Across the Caskey property the wind blew sometimes chill and damp across the Perdido, but the leathery leaves of the water oaks remained in place on the twigs and branches of the ever-taller trees. Moss grew on the trunks, and tiny stunted ferns sprouted in the crotches of the roots, and Zaddie in a long woolen sweater went out early every morning and raked patterns in the sand.

On an afternoon in the early part of October Bray appeared in James Caskey's office, and said, "Mr. James, Miss Mary-Love wants you home right now."

"Bray, I'm coming," said James, and he got up from his desk and walked out of the office without a moment's hesitation. The last time his presence had been so commanded was the afternoon that Elinor had sent his wife away to her death.

"What is it?" said James as he got into the car.

"I don't know," said Bray, who knew perfectly well, but whose instructions had been to say nothing. James understood this, and asked no more questions, although he was very much disturbed. When Bray drew up before Mary-Love's house, James ran up to the front porch, wondering if Grace had been hit on the head with a falling timber in the collapse of her schoolroom roof.

"James!" said Mary-Love in her most musical tone. "We're out here on the porch!"

James stopped dead. Mary-Love's voice bore no hint whatever of disaster, yet there was something in its sweetness, coupled with his summons from the mill and the directive to Bray to say nothing to him, that put James on his guard as if Mary-Love had called out, *Hurry up, James! the most awful thing has happened!*

He slowly mounted the steps, then opened the screened door on to the porch. It was more crowded than usual: Mary-Love sat on the glider with Early Haskew next to her. Sister was on the swing with a little girl beside her. And on the other glider, the one with the chenille blanket thrown over it, sat James's sister-in-law Queenie Strickland and Queenie's son, Malcolm. Malcolm was picking the threads out of a chenille rose. James had not seen any of the Stricklands since his wife's funeral.

"James, I'm so glad you could get away," said Mary-Love. "Queenie came all the way from Nashville to see us!"

Queenie Strickland, who was short and dimpled with bobbed hair that was dyed a shiny black, jumped up and barreled her way toward James, crying out, "Oh, Lord, James Caskey, don't you miss her!"

"I do, I—" But he could say no more, for Queenie had grabbed him around his narrow waist and squeezed the breath right out of him.

"Genevieve was the light of my life! I am miserable without her! I came down to see if you were dead of grief yet!" She released James for a moment and pointed to the glider. "You remember my boy, Malcolm, he was prostrated at his aunt's funeral, say hello to James Caskey, your sweet uncle, boy!"

"Hey, Uncle James," said Malcolm sullenly, and managed at that moment to pick a hole through the chenille spread with his thumbnail.

"And that's my preciousest girl, Lucille, who came down with mumps on the day our darling died and wanted something desperate to come to the funeral but I wouldn't let her even though I had to put her in the hospital in order to get down here in time and one nurse told me she had never heard a child carry on the way that child carried on 'cause she couldn't come to her Aunt Genevieve's funeral!"

Lucille appeared to be about three years old, so she could not have been more than two when Genevieve died. That seemed very young to show such a great interest in the obsequies of even one's closest relatives. However, as if on cue, Lucille burst into tears in the swing, and pulled away with beating fists when Sister attempted to put an arm around her for comfort.

James drew back from Queenie, who had lifted her short arms with the apparent intention of embracing him again. He felt distinctly as if he had fallen into a trap. He looked from Queenie to Mary-Love, as if wondering which of them had been responsible for laying this snare in his unobservant path.

"Well, Queenie," said James after a moment, "did Carl come down here with you?"

Queenie clapped the flat of her hand against her breast, as if to still the sudden beating of her injured heart.

"You have wounded me in speaking of that man!" cried Queenie, staggering backward and waving her other hand carefully behind her to make certain she did not trip over anything.

James stood very still, and was almost certain that he had just stepped into a second pitfall.

Queenie staggered all the way back to the glider, and fell into it heavily. She sat on Malcolm's hand, causing the boy to squeal. He made a great show of his difficulty in extricating his hand from beneath his mother's bulk, then wiggled his fingers to see if they were broken. When he judged them whole, he bunched them into a fist and punched his mother's thigh, but she took no notice at all.

"Mr. Haskew," cried Queenie, "I am sorry!"

"It's all right," said Early automatically, though neither he nor anyone else had any idea why Queenie Strickland should beg his pardon.

93

"You are not family," said Queenie in explanation. "You should not be burdened with the Strickland family troubles."

"You want me to go inside?" said Early amiably, already getting to his feet.

"You sit down," said Mary-Love in a low voice. Then she said more loudly, "Miz Strickland, if you are gone talk family trouble, then I would suggest that you send away these children. I don't particularly want to hear Strickland family tribulations myself, but I certainly don't feel they are fit for the ears of your little boy and your little girl."

"I will not!" cried Queenie. "These children know as much as I do! They have suffered as I have suffered! Has your father beat you, Malcolm Strickland?" she said, turning to her son as if in cross-examination.

"I'll beat him!" cried Malcolm belligerently, and he punched his mother's thigh again.

"Has he touched your pretty angel face, Lucille Strickland?" said Queenie.

Queenie's daughter, who had only just subsided from her previous eruption, suddenly threw her hands up to her face and burst once more into loud sobbing. Sister attempted to draw her hands away, but Lucille wailed so loudly that Sister allowed the tiny hands to snap back into position, so that at least the cries were muffled.

"Carl Strickland," said Queenie in a low, awful voice, "laid his hands on my body. My dress covers the bruises. I would not have you see them for the world. If I had stayed with that man, people in Nashville would have held my name dog-cheap. I will reveal to y'all the greatest mistake that I ever made in my entire life. I will say it out to you, even though there is one of you here who is of no relation whatsoever..." Here she gazed at Early Haskew, and then glanced over the porch in a general sort of way. *"I got into the wrong pew with that man."*

The Caskeys were uncomfortable. Sister would not look at Queenie Strickland, but stared instead at the little girl sitting beside her. Occasionally she attempted to whisper a word or two of consolation. Mary-Love sat stolidly with her arms crossed over her breast and stared at Queenie as if in disbelief that any civilized woman should so disgrace herself. Now and then she glanced up at James reproachfully as if the whole business were his fault. She rather considered that it was, for it was through his marriage that the Caskeys were connected with such a woman as Queenie Strickland. James stood exactly as he stood when he had first stepped onto the porch. He did not know what to do and had no idea what to say and was cognizant of every thought going through Mary-Love's head. In his heart he agreed with her—it was all his fault. All that he might do then was to get the business over with as quickly as possible.

"So you've left Carl, is that what you're saying, Queenie?"

"Of course!" cried Queenie, rising to her feet and apparently preparing to rush James once more. He held up his hands and waved her down again. She fell back onto the glider, but not before Malcolm had another opportunity deliberately to stick his hand beneath her so that he again might have the pleasure of squealing and of administering another punch to his mother's thigh. "Did you want me to stay with him?" cried Queenie. "Did you want to see me beat down into the ground by that devil-man's heavy hand?"

"Oh, Ma, I'd beat him!" cried Malcolm, now administering a volley of illustrative punches against his mother's leg.

"Well," said James, after a moment's thought, "where *is* Carl?"

"Is Carl Strickland in Nashville?" cried Queenie wildly, jumping up and down on the glider. "Do I know? He may be. He may not be. Does Carl Strickland know where *I* am is a better question. He does not. Or if he does, *I* am not the one who told him. I put my bags and my darlings in the back seat of a car and I drove directly to Perdido, Alabama, without a license or ten dollars to my name."

Sister looked up quickly at this mention of money.

Queenie was suddenly quiet. She looked around the porch and when she continued her manner was greatly subdued.

"Do I have a place to go? is another question you might well ask, James Caskey. And what would the answer be, Malcolm Strickland? Would the answer be 'yes'? No, it wouldn't. Would the answer be 'no,' Lucille Strickland? Yes, it would. The Stricklands— except Carl Strickland—are without a roof for their heads. Their automobile is broken down in front of the Perdido town hall, blocking traffic, and will never move again. The Stricklands—except Carl Strickland—don't have the ready cash to purchase themselves a box of rotten apples sold by a colored boy on the side of the highway."

James Caskey collapsed onto the glider between Early Haskew and Mary-Love. For several moments no one said anything, and all that could be heard was the sobbing of Lucille, which had begun anew when her mother had addressed her with the rhetorical question. Ivey Sapp could be seen through the kitchen window that looked out onto the porch, unabashedly watching all that was happening.

"Why exactly did you come to Perdido, Miz Strickland?" asked Mary-Love in a cold voice.

"You have *got* to call me Queenie! You just *got* to! I came to Perdido because of James. I don't have any

96

family. I had Genevieve, and she was all. We were Snyders. All the Snyders are dead. Except my brother Pony Snyder. Pony went to Oklahoma. Married an Indian girl. My darlings here have got fifteen, twenty little Indian cousins now, I hear. But I couldn't go live with Pony. They don't have anything. I don't even know what his Indian wife's first name is. Would I raise my darlings on an Indian reservation?"

"I'd shoot 'em, Ma!" cried Malcolm.

"I know you would, darling," said Queenie indulgently, brushing her son's hair with an affectionate hand. "But I was thinking about all those times my sweet sister stayed with me, and I'd say to her, 'Genevieve Snyder'—I never did get used to her married name, and I guess I'll always think of her as a Snyder—'why are you staying here with me when you've got the best husband in all the world pining away for you down in Perdido? Why aren't you with him?' and she'd say, 'I don't know, 'cause you're right, he's the best man in all the world, he'd do anything for me or for you or for your children. I guess I just love Nashville too much for my own good.' That was her problem, she loved Nashville. I never saw a girl take to a city the way Genevieve took to Nashville. She couldn't be happy anywhere else in the world, I guess. So she told me if anything ever happened and I needed help to come down here and speak to her husband James Caskey, and when something happened—something truly awful—I got in my car and here I am."

Though patently meretricious, Queenie Strickland's speech achieved its desired effect. James Caskey was persuaded to assist her and her children. Their meager baggage was carried into his house by Bray, and later in the afternoon Grace Caskey was introduced to her younger cousins. By way of greeting, Lucille smeared chocolate onto Grace's dress and Malcolm punched her in the stomach.

For the first time in a long while James had dinner served at his own table instead of eating at Mary-Love's. Roxie came back from Elinor's for the evening to cook for them. James had no wish to inflict Queenie and Malcolm and Lucille on the rest of his family. He even took the precaution of sending Grace next door to Mary-Love's, and Mary-Love promised Grace that she could stay for as long as those awful people remained with her father. Over the meal, James said to Queenie, "You sure you want to stay in Perdido? You really think the three of you could be happy here? Here where you don't know anybody?"

"Well, we know you, James Caskey. Who else do we have to know? And now we have been properly introduced to the main part of your family, even though I counted more of 'em at the funeral, I'll probably get to meet 'em all in time, so who else could I want? Lucille and Malcolm are happy as pipers."

Lucille and Malcolm drummed their heels against the rungs of their chairs.

"All right," said James Caskey wearily, regretting that he had ever mourned his loneliness in that house, "then tomorrow I start looking out a place for you to live."

"A place?" cried Queenie, swiveling her head all around, but managing to keep her eye firmly on the gravy boat that she was tilting over her rice. "What is wrong with right here? You have room—all the room in the world! We could have moved our whole entire house inside your front parlor, James Caskey—that's how much room *you* have."

James thought he caught the glint of another trap hidden in the fallen leaves in his path. He stopped stock-still, looked about for alternate routes, and at last said quietly, "No, Queenie."

"James Caskey, you—"

"I will look you out a place to live. I will pay for it, and I will take care of you—within certain limits—for Genevieve's sake. But I cannot let you stay in this house with Grace and me."

"You are lonely!" cried Queenie. James realized, in something of a panic, that he could see a very large trap indeed, just a little farther on in the forest.

"I have Grace!"

"Your darling girl is a tiny child! She cannot keep you company the way I could! We could be a happy family. You have lost your wife—my darling Genevieve—and I have lost a husband, that heathen rapscallion Carl Strickland, I'm ashamed to bear his stinking name! I'm ashamed to have my darlings wear it through life! It's my one comfort—"

"Queenie," said James, interrupting, "you can stay here tonight. But tomorrow I will find someplace else for you to live."

"James Caskey, I know why you are doing this. I know why you are turning me out of your home."

"Why?" he asked, very much puzzled.

"Because darling Malcolm broke that itty-bitty piece of glass this afternoon, he just wanted to look at it, he thought it was so pretty—I did, too, I said, 'Malcolm Strickland, put James's thing back where it belongs and don't you pick up anything in this house ever again,' and he said, 'Ma, I won't ever pick up anything of Uncle James's ever again as long as I live.' I tried to fix it, but those pieces just wouldn't all fit back together again."

James Caskey didn't have the heart to ask what had been broken, and for the next week he was reluctant even to glance at his shelves of beautiful things for fear he would discover which piece the child had destroyed.

"That's not why," he said to Queenie. "I didn't even know about...the accident."

"Ohhh! Then why did I say anything!" cried Queenie involuntarily. "James, we could be so happy!"

But James, displaying uncharacteristic fortitude, would not be persuaded, and next day he bought outright the house next to Dr. Benquith's on the sunny side of the low hill that rose up west of the town hall. It was a merciful ten-minute walk, at the least, from there to the Caskeys' houses, and Queenie was so round and roly-poly that everyone figured that she wouldn't often go to the physical exertion of making that journey. Queenie and her children slept in that house that very first night on rollaway beds appropriated from Mary-Love's storage rooms.

Mary-Love, once she was convinced that James had accepted the blame for having lured Queenie Strickland to Perdido, set out to make the situation as easy as possible for him. She saw to the furniture in one day's shopping in Mobile, thus demonstrating, if anyone had ever doubted, the extent of her procrastination in obtaining the furnishings for Oscar and Elinor's house.

James introduced Oscar and Elinor to Queenie and her children. Something in Elinor's manner, or in her eyes, cowed even Malcolm and Lucille. Malcolm didn't kick and Lucille didn't cry, although when they got home Malcolm showed his mother a bruise on his arm, claiming that Elinor had twisted the flesh there when no one was looking.

Elinor, with the aid of Roxie and Zaddie, ran up curtains for all the windows in Queenie's house, took them over, hung them up, and then went away again without accepting so much as a cup of coffee or piece of cake for their effort.

Queenie didn't have to worry about money, for James Caskey set up small accounts for her in certain stores, and she was allowed to take away what she needed. Once, however, in Berta Hamilton's dress shop, when Queenie pointed out a long coat with a fur collar and wide fur sleeves, Berta Hamilton said pointedly, "Oh, Miz Strickland, I think that's probably not gone fit you too well…"

Queenie insisted on trying it on anyway and, contrary to the prediction, it fit perfectly, and Berta Hamilton was forced to say outright what she had only discreetly hinted at before: "I am not gone put a hundred-and-fifty-dollar coat on Mr. James's bill when you have already spent three hundred and sixty-two dollars in here this month, Miz Strickland."

Queenie fumed, and Queenie fretted, but Queenie went away without the coat. She began to understand what James had meant by "certain limits."

CHAPTER 21

Christmas

Queenie Strickland found that Perdido was a tough
nut to crack. There was no question but that she was
better off than she had been in Nashville; she was
being taken care of in a more agreeable way, she
had a nicer house, and most importantly she had got
rid of her husband, Carl. But other things weren't so
quick in coming; for instance, friends and acquaintances. No woman who talked as much as Queenie
Strickland could get along for any length of time
without people, and she was the sort, moreover, who
rather wore friends down. She needed a number of
them so that she could bear down upon them one by
one a little at a time; that way the abrasions she
inflicted had time to heal and be forgotten. She
wasted no time in building a new circle.

To Florida Benquith next door, Queenie—sweet

as sweet could be—sent over a pie for the doctor and scraps for the dog. The next day she asked Florida if she wouldn't mind setting a hem for her with pins, it would only take three seconds. Florida, envious of the social power wielded by the Caskeys in the town, craftily acquiesced to become Queenie's friend. This, she calculated, would either provide a way of becoming closer with the Caskeys if Queenie ultimately proved herself acceptable to Mary-Love and the rest, or else specifically to annoy them in case Queenie turned out to be an outcast. Thus, Queenie gained a foothold, and from it began deliberately to enlarge her circle of acquaintances. For one thing, she joined the bridge group that met every Tuesday afternoon.

There were two bridge clubs in Perdido, the more fashionable convening on Monday afternoons, the other on the following day; at the second, the principal topic of conversation was what had been said, worn, and served at bridge the day before. The first group centered around Mary-Love; the second revolved around Florida Benquith. Elinor Caskey, when she left Mary-Love's house, and would no longer have anything to do with her mother-in-law, had dropped into the second group. She was rather resented there, first because she carried the greatest social weight, and second because she was a member actually by default. But through these Tuesday afternoon gatherings, Elinor and Queenie became acquainted with each other.

In the middle of November, by the chance of the draw, the Tuesday meetings were held on successive weeks first in Elinor's house and then in Queenie's. Though accidental, this exchange of visits assumed the dimensions of a public embrace, and thereafter Queenie and Elinor were considered to be friends. This was a willful—perhaps even mischievous— misinterpretation of the circumstances on the part of Florida Benquith and her circle, but it was a misinterpretation that stuck, perhaps because neither Queenie nor Elinor did anything to deny it.

Somehow, Mary-Love heard of this, or divined it by miraculous clairvoyance, and was disturbed. Mary-Love had no liking for Queenie, either in her person or in her position as Genevieve's sister. She particularly did not like to see Queenie rollicking behind the enemy lines. She began to fear that Elinor and Queenie would join forces and launch a concerted attack against her.

Consequently, at dinner after church a few weeks later, Mary-Love said to James, "It is time to mend our fences."

James looked up from his plate, surprised. "Have you and I been arguing, Mary-Love? I sure didn't know it, if we were."

"We have not, James, but in case you haven't noticed, most of our family is not speaking."

James—and everyone else at the table—shifted uncomfortably in his chair.

"It is getting close to Christmas," Mary-Love continued, quite as if she bore no responsibility for the estrangements and divisions within the family, "and I think it would be nice if we all spent it together." She paused, perhaps waiting for someone to second this motion. Finding only silence, she went on unperturbed: "We ought to do it for the children, if not for ourselves. There's Grace of course," said Mary-Love, glancing toward her niece across the table, "she's been with us for a while, but now there's Miriam and Frances. And, Lord, they're *sisters,* and they hardly get the chance to look in each other's faces! And now we've got Malcolm and Lucille, they ought to be here—"

"You're inviting Queenie Strickland!" cried Sister in amazement. James just sat with his mouth open.

"I'm inviting the whole *family,*" said Mary-Love,

rather enjoying the consternation she had caused. That she was able to surprise them so completely and to such effect was proof of her continuing power.

"And Oscar and Elinor, too?" asked James, shaking his head in wonder.

"Everybody."

"Do you think they'll come?" wondered Sister. "Queenie will, of course," Sister went on, answering her own question, "and she'll be bound to bring along those two hellions."

"Sister!" cried Mary-Love in reproach, having never heard her daughter speak any word that even approached a curse.

"That's exactly what they are," Sister went on. "But, Mama, you really think you can get Elinor over here, and get her to bring Frances with her?"

"I see no reason why Elinor should not come," said Mary-Love stiffly. "I see no reason why she should not bring her daughter with her. Of course, there is another reason why we are having a party on Christmas."

"What is it?" asked James.

"Early says he is gone have the levee plans done next week. And I think we ought to celebrate his finishing."

"It's taken me a lot longer than I reckoned," explained Early apologetically.

"But he wanted to do it right," said Sister quickly. "And, James, your old council got its money's worth when it hired on Early to do the job. Once he's ready to start, that levee'll go up like nobody's business."

"Well," said James cautiously, "I'm real glad to hear it, but, Mary-Love, I don't think you better say anything about this to Elinor. Don't tell her she's coming over here to a party for the building of the levee—or I can guarantee you she won't step foot in this house."

"You are probably right, James. Maybe if *you* in-

vited her she'd come. Maybe if you told her I'm gone
set up a big tree—the biggest tree we've ever had—
and she can bring all her packages over here, and
tell her we'll fill the whole front parlor with presents
for the children, maybe then she'd be convinced.
Maybe if you could explain to her that the family
ought to be together at Christmas, and maybe if you
told her that Queenie's gone be invited too it'd all
make a big difference."

"She's friends with Queenie now?" said Sister.

Mary-Love nodded. "I've heard tell..."

Sister nodded thoughtfully, suddenly understanding more about Mary-Love's motives for these invitations than Mary-Love would have liked.

Later that afternoon James went over to Elinor's
and invited her and Oscar to Christmas Day at Mary-
Love's. He mentioned Queenie's invitation but said
nothing of Early Haskew's presence, or the fact that
Early was just finishing up his plans for the levee.
Elinor calmly accepted the invitation, merely remarking that she had already planned to go to Mobile to buy everyone presents. At about the same
time Sister went over to Queenie's, taking with her
a plate of hard candy, and extended the same invitation. Queenie desperately tried to think of a way
to discuss with Elinor whether she ought to accept,
but it was imperative that she say yea or nay immediately. She could not plead a prior engagement,
for Sister would know that was a lie. She said yea
and prayed God that she had not offended Elinor in
doing so.

That evening Queenie walked over to Elinor's and
conferred with her new friend upon the matter at
hand. "I could say I had to go back to Nashville for
something or other, and then stay locked up in the
house all day," suggested Queenie with some enthu-
siasm, confident that the idea was so ridiculous that
Elinor would never encourage her to go through with

107

it. It had been for Elinor's sake alone that Queenie had declared an aversion to Mary-Love.

"No," said Elinor, "Oscar and I are going, and we're taking Frances, so there's no reason why you shouldn't go too, Queenie."

"I'm glad you said that," said Queenie. "'Cause it makes everything a whole lot easier for everybody."

"I *want* to go," said Elinor. "I haven't been in that house for a long while, and I think it's time that I saw what Miss Mary-Love has been up to."

In the first part of November, a draftsman from Pensacola had taken up residence in the Osceola Hotel, and worked day and night for three weeks, producing final drawings, on blueprint paper, of all Early's plans for the levee. On the day that he finished, Sister and Early took the plans home and spread them out one by one on Sister's bed, and admired them. The next day the blueprints were taken to the records office at the town hall and photographed for safety's sake. Then the following Tuesday, Early took them before the town council, along with his revised estimates of costs and a timetable for completion of various stages of the work. To the council's satisfaction, the cost was lower than originally predicted, and if all went well, Perdido would be completely protected by an impervious, indestructible levee by the winter of 1924.

Tom DeBordenave reported what everyone on the council already knew—that the state legislature had authorized a bond issue for the construction and that the sales of these bonds would be handled through the First National Bank of Mobile. Each of the millowners had already deposited twenty-five thousand dollars in the Perdido bank, and nothing now stood in the way of the work's immediate commencement.

By unanimous consent of the council, Early Haskew was appointed principal engineer for the project, and was directed to go down to Pensacola and Mobile and up to Montgomery immediately, and to begin speaking to contractors and asking for sealed bids. The meeting closed with a prayer. With bowed head, James Caskey asked God to send no more high water before Early Haskew was finished with his work.

Early set forth immediately on his mission, and was sorely missed by Sister. But she and Mary-Love were busy with preparations for the Christmas party, the event having added to the usual amount of activity before the holiday.

There was now increased traffic between Mary-Love's and Elinor's houses. Elinor sent over a jar of strawberry preserves; this favor was returned in the form of two pounds of shelled pecans; which offering came back as a fruitcake soaked in pre-Prohibition Havana rum. Such tokens continued to be passed back and forth between Ivey's kitchen and Roxie's kitchen, growing more valuable in each journey across the yard in Zaddie's arms.

Still, Mary-Love and Sister saw no more of Elinor than they had in previous months. In fact, neither of them set eyes upon Elinor until one day about a week before Christmas. Sister had gone over to Elinor's with a great box of infant clothing, things outgrown by Miriam but which might, she thought, be of some use for Frances. Elinor thanked Sister for her thoughtfulness, asked her inside, served her Russian tea, allowed her to hold Frances and coo over her, and gave her an armful of wrapped gifts to take home and place under the tree.

Early had hoped to be away no more than a week, but twice he sent telegrams to say he had been forced to go farther afield than he had hoped would be necessary. "I don't imagine he's gone make it for Christmas," said Mary-Love to disappointed Sister. "That's all right with me. It means we'll just be plain family."

Nevertheless, on Christmas Eve, Sister sat in the window of her room for three hours watching out for Early's arrival. But since the engineer didn't own an automobile, there was little hope of his driving up in one, and there was no other means by which he could get down from the train station in Atmore. At last Mary-Love came into Sister's room and demanded that she go to bed. Sister did so, rather than admit to her mother the cause of her anxiety.

At first, everything seemed to go as well as anyone could have wished. The doors of the parlor had been shut against any early intrusions by the children. After a breakfast that seemed interminable to Grace and Malcolm and Lucille doors were opened and the presents were revealed in all their shining array. Grace clapped her hands and gazed rapturously at the tiers of fancily wrapped gifts that were terraced out from the base of the tree until the whole parlor was nearly filled with them. There were gifts under chairs, lurking behind the curtains, placed on windowsills, stacked on the mantel, and piled on the sofa. Besides these, several large unwrapped gifts stood in the corners of the room—a rocking horse for Lucille, a red bicycle for Malcolm, and a turreted dollhouse, filled with furniture, for herself. The Caskeys sat wherever they could find places in the crowded room, and a few of the dining room chairs were brought up to the open doorway. Zaddie and Ivey and Roxie, who had worked all morning in the kitchen, cleared the dining room and then sat together on a window seat there, from which vantage point they could watch the proceedings and receive the gifts intended for them.

It was Grace's duty to pick up each present, read the card attached, and hand it out. Malcolm demanded that he be allowed to assist, but since he could not yet read, he had to satisfy himself with distributing the gifts as Grace called out the names. Because of the number of presents involved, this was a slow process and Grace was inclined to make it even more so, often not passing out the next gift before the last had been opened. Everyone got plenty of presents, and soon the parlor was a sea of discarded paper and tissue and ribbon, in the midst of which were neatly stacked islands of gifts, with the cards carefully preserved. The air was thick with exclamations of surprise, gratitude, admiration, and good-natured envy. Grace was certain she had never been so happy in her life.

The only gifts not distributed were those intended for Early Haskew. These, without even calling out his name, Grace simply set to one side.

The merriment continued for more than two hours. Before the end of it, Roxie and Ivey returned to the kitchen to start cooking dinner. The telephone rang once. Sister, nearest it, went to answer. Hearing the voice on the other end, she immediately turned away, and carried the telephone out of sight behind the staircase.

It was Early Haskew, calling from the train station in Atmore. He apologized for not being able to get there sooner, regretted disturbing everyone on Christmas morning, but wondered if someone might not be sent up to Atmore to fetch him. As soon as he had hung up Sister went into the kitchen where Bray sat at the table opening the first of four gifts that had been under the tree for him. He was already wearing his best uniform, and at Sister's behest went immediately to get out the automobile.

Sister said nothing of this when she returned to the living room. Mary-Love was so deeply involved with the opening of the gifts and the delight of the children that she forgot to ask Sister who it was that had telephoned.

Early Haskew walked into the house an hour later. Grace and Lucille were in the front parlor with their toys and the tree; Malcolm was outside riding his new bicycle up and down the street; the servants were all working on dinner in the kitchen; and the adult Caskeys, with the two infants, were sitting around the dining table once again.

At the unexpected sight of Early Haskew, Mary-Love emitted a little scream of delight and Queenie began to talk at the rate of a mile a minute to no one in particular. Oscar and James rose with exclamations of surprise and delight, shook hands with him cordially and pulled a chair up to the table for him. Sister, holding Miriam, and Elinor, holding Frances, said nothing. Sister wore a fixed, almost idiotic smile, while Elinor seemed troubled and distracted.

Early sat down at the head of the table and spoke to everyone in turn in his loud, measured voice. He was glad to see James and Oscar again and he had lots of things to tell them and talk over with them. He was very happy to be back in Mary-Love's house and she couldn't have any idea how much he had missed it. He called out to Ivey Sapp in the kitchen that nobody in Mobile, Montgomery, Pensacola, Natchez, or New Orleans cooked anything like the way that she cooked. Yes, he remembered Miz Strickland very well and Bray had nearly run down her little boy in the street on his new red wheel. He didn't know how he got along without Sister for so long because she always told him what he should be doing and it was sure lonely in those places and he was always turning around to say something to Sister and lo and behold she just wasn't there, and—

more quietly—how was Miss Elinor doing, and wasn't her baby just looking *fine?*

Elinor nodded briefly, but did not say a word.

After Early's greetings, Oscar wanted to know what Early had managed to accomplish. Out of deference to his wife, he did not say the words "on the levee," but it was evident, from a tightening of Elinor's mouth, that those words needn't be spoken aloud for her to know perfectly well to what her husband referred.

"Well," said Early, "I tell you, I think I found somebody. I looked all over, I talked to two thousand people—or almost—and I found a man in Natchez who is willing to come here and submit a bid. What I would do if I was the town council is accept his bid even if it's not the lowest. This man—whose name is Avant, Morris Avant—is gone do you the best job. When you've got a job as big as this levee, then you gone want..."

Seeing Oscar cringe as he spoke, Early paused. Oscar had turned and looked at his wife at the other end of the table. Everyone else did too. Elinor's head was lowered, and she was buttoning Frances's little chemise. If she had a telling expression upon her face, no one could see it to read it.

"...a job like this levee," Early went on cautiously, "then you gone want to have it done right."

"I'm going to take Frances upstairs for a nap," said Elinor suddenly. "She can hardly keep her eyes open. Miss Mary-Love, where should I put her?"

"Put her in Miriam's bed, Elinor. Wait, I'll come up with you."

"Oh no, you stay down here. I'll be back down in a bit." Elinor rose and silently walked out of the dining room, into the hallway, and up the stairs to the second floor.

Everyone at the table knew that Elinor had left because of Early Haskew's presence and his talk of the building of the levee. The curious thing was, however, that Elinor had not done more. She had not taken Frances home, she had only gone upstairs with her. She had not said *I will not allow myself to be in the same room with that man,* she had said *I'll be back down in a bit.* She had hidden her anger behind a mask of polite impassivity. Mary-Love and Sister took deep breaths together and exhaled slowly.

"Will wonders never cease?" asked Sister softly.

"I thought it was gone be up with us," said Mary-Love.

Queenie, for once, sat still and quiet—like one watching a battle from a protected place, anxious to learn which army would win, to which general she would soon swear allegiance.

Elinor did not reappear for the next hour, and for the next hour Early talked of his trip. In the meantime, Roxie came in and began to set the table for dinner. By the time that Early was finished with his chronicle, it was time to call the children in. Miriam had already been fed, and was taken upstairs by Mary-Love and placed in a little fortress of pillows on Sister's bed. Mary-Love then knocked on the door of Miriam's nursery, softly opened the door and told Elinor, who was seated in a chair by the window looking out at the muddy Perdido, that dinner was ready downstairs if she was ready too. Elinor declared that she had been thinking of her family and the place she had come from and had forgot the time. On the way out, Mary-Love peered over into the crib, and exclaimed, "Frances is the prettiest baby I ever did see—except for Miriam of course!"

Christmas dinner was more formal than breakfast. The infants were sleeping upstairs and the three other children had been banished to a small square red deal table set up in the kitchen, where all three acutely felt the disgrace of their tender

114

ages. Thus the adults had the dining room to themselves, and when they were all milling about the table unsure of where to sit, Mary-Love pointed out places for them all, taking care that Early and Elinor sat as far apart as possible. Having engineered the insult of bringing them together at all, she could afford to be charitable on this small point.

After the blessing, recited by James sitting between Elinor and Queenie, Sister turned to Early, seated beside her, and said, "So, so far as you're concerned, everything is pretty much set?"

"Well, yes," said Early. "Why do you ask?"

"Because then I have something to say," said Sister.

But just at that moment Ivey and Roxie brought in a turkey, half of which had already been carved in the kitchen, a pheasant shot by Oscar on Caskey land in Monroe County, a plate of fried mullet, a small ham, a sweet potato casserole, bowls of little green peas, creamed corn, stuffing, black-eyed peas and ham hocks, boiled okra, pickle relish, a plate of Parker House rolls, a plate of biscuits, a mold of ice-cold butter with a design of a Christmas tree on top, and a pitcher of iced tea. James was given the ham to carve and Oscar the pheasant.

With the arrival of the food, no one showed any great curiosity to know what Sister had to say; in any case she was used to her concerns being accorded precious little worth. When at last everyone had filled his plate and the platters had been removed to the sideboard and Zaddie had taken away the biscuits and replaced the cooled rolls with hot, Mary-Love said, "So what is it you are dying to say, Sister? I never saw a grown woman twitch so!"

"Has everybody been served now?" asked Sister sarcastically.

"Yes," said Mary-Love, apparently unaware of the

115

tone in her daughter's voice. "So will you please get on with it?"

"Well," said Sister, gazing around the table and disregarding the fact that every head was bowed over a plate and not even bothering to glance up at her, "now that everything is set on the levee, so far as Early is concerned, he and I are gone get married."

Everyone looked up. Everyone put down his fork and stared at Sister. Everyone then turned and looked at Early. Everyone in fact half-suspected that Sister had made it up and that Early would appear as amazed as anybody.

But Early was grinning, and he said loudly, "Sister doesn't care *how* loud I snore!"

Mary-Love pushed her plate away, saying tartly, "Sister, I *do* wish you and Oscar wouldn't tell me things like this during dinner. I tell you, it takes my appetite right away and there's nothing I can do to get it back. Roxie!" she called. Roxie appeared in the doorway. "Roxie, take away my plate. I am not gone be able to eat another bite." Roxie came and took the plate. "Early," said Mary-Love, turning to the engineer who sat at her right hand, "is this true, are you gone marry my little girl?"

"Yes, ma'am," said Early proudly.

"I don't believe it," returned Mary-Love. "Did she ask you, or did you ask her?"

"I asked her, she—"

By this time, the others at the table had regained their composure, and Early's reply to Mary-Love was lost beneath a welter of congratulations. James spoke for all, perhaps, when he remarked, with no thought of unkindness, "Sister, I never thought I'd see the day!"

"When *is* the day?" asked Mary-Love suddenly.

Early's eyebrows shot up. He had no idea. He turned to Sister. Sister said: "Thursday week. The third of January."

"Oh, you cain't, Sister!" cried Mary-Love. "You got to put it off, you got—"

"Thursday week," repeated Sister, quite as loudly as her fiancé might have spoken. She turned to her mother, smiled her bland smile and said, "Mama, you tricked Oscar into putting off, and all it got you was trouble. You're not gone have a word to say about it this time."

"I am *ashamed*," said Mary-Love vehemently, "to have people sit at my table and listen to my child talk to her mother that way."

"They can leave if they want to," said Sister indifferently. "Or, Mama, you can leave. Or I can leave and take Early with me. Or we can all just sit here and finish our dinner. Merry Christmas, y'all."

The assembled table thought they had never seen such a hardness in Sister. They looked at her and at Early, and wondered if the engineer knew what kind of bargain he had made.

Sister called to Roxie and told her to bring Mary-Love's plate back. "Mama," said Sister grimly, "this is a happy day for me, and you are not gone spoil it by sending back your plate to the kitchen. You are gone sit still in your place and be happy for me, you hear?"

Mary-Love spent the next half hour gnawing at a wing of the pheasant. Sister, meanwhile, gave a little account of her wooing by Early, and remarked that everything had been settled between them for more than a month and had only waited the completion of his plans for the levee to be announced properly.

Mary-Love didn't say another word, but once or twice she glanced at Elinor. Elinor always caught those glances and returned them with a little satisfied half-smile. Mary-Love had been bested by the very weapon she had attempted to employ against Elinor—Early Haskew. Elinor asked what Mary-

Love dared not ask: "Sister," Elinor said, "where are you going to be living after you and Mr. Haskew get married? Are you going to stay on here, or are you planning to pack up and move out and leave Miss Mary-Love all by herself?"

CHAPTER 22

The Spy

Sister would not be put off, Sister would not be persuaded. Mary-Love begged that she be allowed to have a half-decent wedding for at least *one* of her children, but Sister said briskly, "Will it take more than a month to arrange?"

"*Anything* half-decent would take at least three months, Sister, you know that! We would have to—"

"Then Early and I are getting married next week," said Sister.

Mary-Love would have liked to put up a fight, but Sister made it clear that she would take no part in such an altercation. She intended to marry Early Haskew, and her mother's objection to any part of such a proceeding would only serve to drive Sister away.

Mary-Love was bewildered. She had intended

Christmas to be the first step in a major campaign mounted against Elinor and Elinor's ally Queenie. Instead she had found herself attacked by an army—Sister's—she had not even known was in the field. Caught by surprise, she could do nothing but perform a strategic surrender. Her consolation had to be that she was inducting into her family a soldier—Early Haskew—who was inimical to her enemy.

The ceremony was held in Mary-Love's front parlor, where there were still needles in the carpet from the Christmas tree. The Methodist minister officiated, and Grace was a combination bridesmaid and flower girl. Sister had debated about whether to ask Elinor to be her matron of honor, but knowing with what disgust Elinor viewed her fiancé—or at least her fiancé's purpose in the town—Sister decided not to risk the embarrassment of a refusal.

For a wedding gift James and Mary-Love went in together and bought Early an automobile—just such a one as James had heard him admire on the street one day. In this new automobile, directly after the ceremony, Sister and Early took off for Charleston, South Carolina, a city Sister had never visited but had always wanted to see. After they were gone, Mary-Love sighed her biggest sigh, then sat down at a corner of the dining room table and tilted her head until it came to rest horizontally on the upraised palm of her hand.

"What's wrong with you, Mary-Love?" said Queenie, who, for the ceremony, had got permission from James to purchase a sea green silk dress at Berta Hamilton's. "Don't you know you have now got one of the finest son-in-laws in all the state of Alabama south of Montgomery?"

"I do know it, Queenie," sighed Mary-Love loudly, as if she intended those still in the front parlor to hear her words. "What I just cain't understand is the way I am treated by my children."

"You have *fine* children. Your children could squeeze you to death with their love."

"Well, that's how I feel about *them*. They don't care much for me, though."

"Of course we do, Mama," said Oscar, who *had* heard his mother from the parlor and had come in to pronounce his undiminished affection.

"If you really loved me," said Mary-Love, still loudly for Elinor and James remained in the next room, "would you have gotten married in James's living room one afternoon when I was down in Mobile shopping? Would Elinor have stood up in front of a female preacher wearing a dress that was only basted together? Would you two have driven away on a honeymoon before I had the chance to kiss you on the mouth and say how happy I was?" Mary-Love had raised her head to the vertical again, and now was speaking these words savagely. "If Sister had loved me, would she have contracted an engagement and kept it secret until she could spring it on me at the dinner table on Christmas Day? Would she have gotten married one week later, when she could just as easily have waited a couple of months and made me happy by it? Would she have invited nobody but the family, when we could have sent out invitations and gotten three hundred people to travel by automobile from Montgomery and by train from Mobile, and *filled* the church?"

"Mama," said Oscar, unmoved by either the loving reproach of her words or the angry reproach of her voice, "you didn't want Elinor and me to get married at all. You put off and put off, until we *had* to do it behind your back. That's what Sister was thinking of. She didn't want you to start with her, that's all. She thought you had an ulterior motive in wanting a church wedding three months from now."

121

Mary-Love sighed again and said, "Go away, Oscar. You don't love me."

"I do, Mama," said Oscar softly, and he walked out of the room.

Sister had never said where she and Early intended to live when they returned from their honeymoon. Mary-Love was in a perfect agony to know, but she had never dared put that question to her daughter. Just asking would have given Sister a tremendous advantage in any subsequent bargaining in the matter. Mary-Love was by no means a stupid woman, and she understood perfectly that for all their rebelliousness—exhibited principally in the manner of their marriages—Oscar and Sister loved her. Their high-handedness was a tactic they had learned from Mary-Love herself. Oscar, being a man, had learned it only imperfectly, and had needed Elinor to prod him. Sister had swallowed the lessons whole, and had dragged Early Haskew will-he nill-he to the altar. Though she would never have admitted it, Mary-Love was actually proud of her daughter for doing what she had done. By her sudden marriage Sister had attained adulthood in Mary-Love's eyes; she was within striking distance of equality. And now more than ever before, Mary-Love dreaded losing her, dreaded to be alone in the house; she even declared to herself that she would miss Early Haskew's loud voice and terrible snoring.

And then there was Miriam to consider; the child belonged to Mary-Love and Sister jointly. It was inconceivable that Sister would attempt to take the child away with her—and almost as difficult for Mary-Love to imagine how she could manage the child on her own. The only solution, it seemed to Mary-Love, was that Sister and Early should remain in the house. Therefore, while Sister and Early were away on honeymoon, Mary-Love drove down to Mobile and picked out the most expensive suite of bedroom furniture she could find. She moved Sister's furniture out of the front bedroom and repainted the walls. She installed a new carpet, then filled the room with the vast new suite. She even went so far as to knock on Elinor's door and ask if Elinor might consider running up a new set of draperies for Sister's homecoming. Elinor, to Mary-Love's considerable surprise, agreed readily. She even offered to purchase the fabric, but Mary-Love had already taken care of this.

The draperies were sewn that evening and hung the next day. Mary-Love thanked Elinor, and accepted her daughter-in-law's invitation to take supper with her and Oscar. For the first time, Mary-Love ate a meal in the house she had built for her son and his wife. Miriam, nearly two, was placed in a high chair brought over earlier by Zaddie, and throughout the meal eyed her real mother with a mixture of curiosity and suspicion.

A few days later, Sister and Early returned. She kissed Mary-Love hello, and before she had even taken off her hat she exclaimed, "Mama, I smell new furniture! Have you been down in Mobile again?" Then Mary-Love took her upstairs and showed her what had been accomplished in her absence.

Early, a simple man, remembered that Sister had said that very little would give her greater pleasure than to leave her mother high and dry. He had therefore assumed that upon their return from honeymoon, they would find another place to live. This newly furnished room puzzled him, as did the expression on Sister's face.

"It's real pretty, isn't it, Early?" Sister asked.

He nodded, asking, "Is this where we're gone be living?"

Sister looked at her mother. "For the time being,"

Sister said. "Mama, it's real pretty, you went to a lot of trouble."

Mary-Love now knew several things. First was that, despite "for the time being," Sister had no intention of leaving the house; and second, that she never had such an intention, the appearance she had given of having decided to leave her mother had been merely a feint. In this, Mary-Love thought she saw a little too much of herself. Sister knew what she was doing, and it was to an equal that Mary-Love replied, "Of course I went to some trouble, Sister! I had to do *something* to keep you with me! What would I have done if you and Early had wanted to find someplace else to live? What would we have done with poor old Miriam? Would we have cut her in two with a sword? Would we have given her back to Elinor?"

"Couldn't give up Miriam! But, Mama," warned Sister, unwilling completely to give up the edge she had attained, "don't go getting too used to having Early and me around. You never know when we'll up and leave you high and dry!"

"Oh, you wouldn't do that to your poor old mama," said Mary-Love softly, then left them to unpack.

Several contractors to whom Early had spoken the month before submitted sealed bids for the construction of the levee, and Early's choice for the job, Morris Avant, had the next-to-lowest. On Early's recommendation, Avant was awarded the first part of the contract.

But a great deal had to be accomplished before actual work on the levee could begin. The construction would require the services of between one hundred fifty and two hundred men, and though some might be unskilled and drawn from the unemployed ranks of Baptist Bottom, most were going to have to be imported. When the water pumping station had been built the year after the flood of 1919, twenty-five workers had been brought in. The foremen had stayed at the Osceola Hotel and the lower-paid workers had camped out on the stage of the school auditorium and been fed in the school kitchen on weekdays and at the Methodist Church on Saturdays and Sundays. This arrangement was hardly sufficient or appropriate for a near-army of men. Someone suggested housing the men in the schools, but depriving the schools of the use of the buildings for nearly two years wasn't really to be thought of seriously. So in a field just south of Baptist Bottom, the Hines brothers went to work putting up two large buildings for the accommodation of white workers, one a dormitory, and the other a kitchen and dining room.

Perdido citizens began to realize to what extent the levees would alter the aspect of their town. In the short term, it would mean the influx of workers and the expenditure of money, which was bad enough; but now they began to think about what it was going to be like to be hemmed in with walls of dirt for the remainder of their lives; to look out their windows and see not the rivers flowing past but only red walls of clay higher than their houses, wide and stolid and unhandsome. Some remembered how Elinor Caskey had spoken out against the levees, saying just some such thing, and had spoken even though her own husband was one of the prime movers in the business.

People now began to ask Elinor's opinion of the plans that had been made, and the preparations that were afoot, but Elinor would only say, "I told everybody what I thought. I still think it. By the time the levees are finished—if they *are* ever finished—it will be like living in an old clay quarry. Levees can wear down, and levees can wash away. Levees can spring holes, and levees can crack wide open. There's nothing that's ever going to stop the flow of a river when it wants to flow down to the sea, and there's nothing that can keep water from rising when it wants to spill over the top of a mound of clay."

Elinor wasn't to be meddled with during these days. There was something volatile in her temper, in her manner, and in her opinions. Her supper invitation to Mary-Love was not repeated, and though she had made curtains for Sister and Early's marriage chamber, she never even so much as welcomed them back from their honeymoon.

One day when Mary-Love was visiting Creola Sapp, down with some sort of winter fever, she found Creola's youngest child crawling about the floor wearing a dress that she, Mary-Love, had made for Miriam a year earlier. The garment had been one of the many articles of baby clothing that she had turned over to Elinor for the use of Frances, and which Elinor had accepted with apparent gratitude.

"Oh, yes, ma'am," said Creola, when questioned, "Miss El'nor good to me, bring me out a whole box of things for Luvadia. Prettiest things you ever saw!"

"I'll say they are, Creola. I'll just say they are!" murmured Mary-Love, furious that Elinor would give all those fine things away to Creola Sapp. She was even more distressed about Elinor's action because it had been discovered by merest accident — that is to say, it had not been done simply for effect. To Mary-Love, to do a thing not merely for effect argued a perversity in Elinor's character. It quite took away Mary-Love's breath.

Mary-Love rushed home and ran upstairs to Sister, who was in the nursery with Miriam. Mary-Love waxed indignant over the notion of those fine clothes going directly from their precious Miriam, *two years old, and she cried unless there was a tiny diamond bracelet clapped around her wrist*, to Luvadia Sapp, *a fat grinning morsel of alligator bait crawling*

126

around on the splintery boards of a crumbling shack in the piney woods. "I cain't understand why Elinor would do a thing like that!" cried Mary-Love, but included in her frustration was her inability to understand *anything* her daughter-in-law did.

Sister's teeth went *clack-clack*. She said, "Mama, Elinor is upset."

"What have I done now?"

"Elinor's not upset because of you, Mama. She's upset because they have started to work on the levee, and she hates that levee the way you and I hate hell and the Republicans."

Mary-Love looked first at Sister, then out the window at Elinor's house as if that facade, perhaps in the configuration of draperies opened and draperies closed, might provide confirmation of Sister's thesis. Then she glanced down at Miriam toddling gravely across the rug, and said, "Sister, I think you may be right about that."

Frances caught a bit of a cold late in February, a little cold that Roxie said was no more than any child could suffer at that time of the year and at her time of life. Dr. Benquith saw the child and agreed with Roxie. Despite the reassurances, Elinor insisted that the child was in danger of her very life. She told Oscar that for the time being she would sleep in the nursery in case the child should experience difficulty in breathing. Oscar, who could scarcely bring himself to argue against the well-being of his daughter, acquiesced to this. A cot was set up in the nursery and Elinor abandoned her husband's bed.

Frances, to all appearances, soon got over the cold, but Elinor continued to stay with her day and night. Mary-Love and Sister next door speculated that Elinor remained as close to the child as she did not for Frances's protection and comfort, but rather so that no one might discern that the child was totally

127

recovered. In any case, Frances's illness, whether supposed or real, went on and on, and it kept Elinor indoors. Her only foray into Perdido society was her Tuesday bridge games, and these she insisted be held, ignoring rotation, in her own home for the duration of the child's danger.

Queenie Strickland saw more of Elinor than anyone else. Queenie believed in Frances's illness, mainly because it seemed politic to do so. She frequently passed on to Elinor magazine articles that gave precise instructions for the care of ailing infants. She purchased little bottles of quackery at the pharmacy, tied the necks with pink ribbons, and waved them like a pendulum in Frances's face. She came daily to ask after the child, and to relate to Elinor the progress of the levee. From Queenie alone did Elinor accept such news, and as the two women sat in the swing on the second-floor porch, Elinor gazed out through the screens at the Perdido and listened tight-lipped as Queenie spoke: "Yesterday afternoon Sister was down in Baptist Bottom, and on the spot she hired three colored women to work in the kitchen. They gone get two dollars a day and not gone do nothing in this world but cook for seventy-five men. I wish *I* got paid like that for cooking for Malcolm and Lucille! Then over at the mill, they tore down those little store-buildings that are right on the edge of the river, and some other men were there building 'em right back up again except thirty feet back, and this time they are putting in windows 'cause those buildings are so hot in the summer that the men cain't hardly stand to go in there. And Mr. Avant and Early rode out to Mr. Madsen's—where Mary-Love gets her potatoes?—and told him they'd pay him two dollars for every wagonload of dirt they took out from behind his house. Y'see, he's got this mound right in back of his house—they say it's Indian burying ground and some old Indian bones are laying at the bottom of it pro'bly, and Mr. Madsen says if they find the bones they got to take them away with everything else. He says he was planning to clear it off and plant potatoes back there anyway, but he'll take the two dollars if they offer it to him, he's not proud..."

Because Elinor never objected to hearing these things, and because she had once cautioned Queenie not to tell anyone that she listened to them, Queenie understood that it had become her duty to find out everything there was to know about the building of the levee and to report it directly to Elinor. It was as if Elinor had been a proud sovereign, and the levee builders of Perdido had been her subjects raising earthen barricades and fomenting rebellion. Queenie was the loyal spy who reported every movement of the rabble so that her sovereign might know everything and yet still maintain the appearance of being above such small considerations.

The Hines brothers continued work on the dormitory and dining room for the expected workers. Early and Sister went around Baptist Bottom knocking on doors looking for people in need of employment. Every Thursday the Perdido *Standard* was filled with long articles detailing the preparations under way for the construction of the levee, always including at least one photograph of Early Haskew. In general, the town wound itself up very tightly in preparation for the very first wagonload of dirt to be spilled out onto the bank of the Perdido River. As all these events were rumbling along with ever-increasing speed and ever-increasing noise, Elinor Caskey kept more and more to her own house, and was never seen anywhere near the construction.

CHAPTER 23

Queenie's Visitor

Work on the levee began on the Baptist Bottom bank of the Perdido south of the junction. Early hired men in Pensacola, Mobile, Montgomery, and even from as far away as Tallahassee, to come and live for a year or so in the dormitory. Quarries in three counties were widened and deepened as stone and earth were extracted and loaded onto trucks or mule wagons. Every morning these vehicles lumbered into town along each of the three roads by which Perdido was accessible to the rest of the civilized world. A few small houses had been razed in Baptist Bottom and the first loads of dirt dropped there, the loose earth packed and molded by an army of colored men with spanking-new shovels. This first wall of clay seemed no more than a child's mud castle raised to enormous and ridiculous size, so that everyone wondered if so fragile-seeming an embankment *could* hold against the river if it took it in its mind to rise?

Every day the local colored population gathered and watched for hours with never-failing interest as the same actions and motions were performed over and over again: a wagon pulled up, dirt and clay were unloaded, dirt and clay were raised to the top of the mound under the direction of an overseer, dirt and clay were tamped into place. On the other side of the river, in the field behind the town hall, an equal number of idle white people gathered and gawked equally hard. Both groups of spectators declared that it was such a slow and such a massive job that there could be no hope of its being finished within their children's lifetimes. Perhaps Early Haskew was a great confidence man and nothing more. Hadn't they better stop the business right now?

A month or so later, one of the early morning gawkers behind the town hall looked across the Perdido and seemed to see the earthwork with new eyes. Previously, the mound of earth on the Baptist Bottom shore had seemed shapeless and amorphous to this man; but this day, in the morning air, without much actual change from the morning before, it seemed a gaudy vision of what the whole rampart would eventually be. This man, astounded by his sudden visionary extrapolation, pointed out what he saw to the next gawker. The second man was even more astonished, for he saw it too, and he had been one of the levee's most vociferous detractors. The word—or rather the vision—spread, from man to man and from woman to woman throughout Perdido, and everyone went over to Baptist Bottom and looked at the thing up close, and actually applauded Early Haskew when he drove up in his automobile. Suddenly the levee had become a great thing in Perdido.

This remarkable rampart was twenty-five feet

wide at its base, about twenty-two feet high—depending upon the part of town—and about twelve feet broad at the top. With every fifty feet or so of the levee that was completed, a layer of topsoil was added to the top and sides, and immediately planted with grass. Black women in the community made forays into the forests and dug up smilax, small dogwoods, hollies, and wild roses, which were also planted in the red clay walls. Further to guard against erosion, Early had slips of kudzu placed at the base of the levee on both sides in great holes filled with pulverized cow manure. He had been assured that no amount of fertilizer could burn the roots of that rampaging vine.

Early and Morris Avant conferred every day, and Morris pointed out that the speed with which the levee could be built was in direct proportion to the number of men they had working on it. Early did a little figuring and a little more talking with Morris Avant and his foremen, then went back to the town council and asked whether they wouldn't authorize money for the building of another dormitory to house more workers. The cost would be offset by the overhead expenses saved in the quicker completion of the project. Early was told to do whatever he saw fit, and the Hines brothers went to work the next day.

Early did not worry about finding workers now to fill that dormitory, for it had become known all over south Alabama, south Mississippi, and the Florida panhandle that wages, room, and board were to be had in Perdido. So when the Hines brothers finished the second dormitory, and two more colored women had been hired on to help in the kitchens, every man in search of work on the levee was accommodated. They drifted in from God-knew-where, appearing suddenly out of the forest or entering town on the buckboard of a wagon bringing in clay or simply trudging in on the road from Atmore. They all went by nicknames, and none seemed to possess a history entirely unblemished.

These men worked so hard all day that it was a wonder that they had the energy, after the sun went down, to sit up for their meals in the dormitory kitchen. But the men ate voraciously, and seemed not to know the word "weariness." At night, even more so than during the day, Perdido seemed to have been invaded by these men; people now locked their doors. The levee-men were rowdy, and they consumed vast quantities of the liquor brewed up on Little Turkey Creek. Two little Indian girls on a swayback mule brought in ten gallons of the stuff each day and sold it at the dormitories every morning before school, entrusting the proceeds to their teacher until school was over. A gambling den run by Lummie Purifoy opened in Baptist Bottom; his ten-year-old daughter Ruel passed her evening serving rotgut liquor by the tin-cupful. Two white women, it was whispered, had been driven up from Pensacola by a colored man in a yellow coat. They were the very *lowest* sort of white women, and actually rented a house in Baptist Bottom. The door of that house, it was said, was never closed to a man who knocked on it with a silver dollar in his fist. Perdido's three policemen tried to stay away from these purlieus of the levee-men at night; even with their pistols, they were no match for one hundred and seventy-five powerful, brawling drunks. It was a mercy that, after dark, these men tended to keep to themselves. Only occasionally might three or four of them be seen reeling up Palafox Street, leaning against store windows with closed drunken eyes; and once in a while they made nuisances of themselves in the audience at the Ritz Theater with rude noises and obscene commentary on the movies. Very occasionally a black man would have to bar his door and plead pitifully for the purity of his daughter while the daughter ran deftly out the back way.

Yet the white workers—no-good, unpleasant, and possibly dangerous—were a necessary evil. They would go away after a year or so, but the levee they built would protect Perdido for an eternity.

It was the summer of 1923, and the whole town seemed to stink with the sweat of the levee-men. The construction on the eastern bank of the Perdido had been finished. Two sets of concrete steps had been built into the sides of the levee, and a track had been beaten into the earth along the top. This was a favorite promenade of the colored population after church on Sunday, and colored children played there all day. From the windows of the town hall, the levee was a bright red wall, and after a rain it became shining red and was a dominant feature of the landscape.

Work had begun just behind the town hall now, and before long it would seem as if the Perdido below the junction were flowing meekly through a deep red gully. Already the river seemed to have surrendered much of its former belligerence and pride.

Beneath the constant heat, the workers were wearier than before, but instead of dampening their spirit at night, the warm weather seemed to cause them to drink more and to carouse with greater vehemence and noise. On these summer nights, when respectable Perdido sat on its porch for air after supper, the racket made by the workers on the far side of the river was a distant but very audible roar, punctuated occasionally by a coherent shout. Perdido rocked grimly, and fanned its face, and said in a low voice, *I sure will be glad when those men have gone back to wherever it was they came from.* And to be on the safe side, hunting guns that usually weren't taken out until deer season were cleaned and loaded

135

and propped in the corner behind the front door. The unspoken fear was that the two white women from Pensacola who had taken up scandalous residence in Baptist Bottom would prove insufficient for the "needs" of the workers.

One night, in the midst of the heat—and the rocking, and the fanning, and the worry—the telephone rang in Oscar Caskey's house about ten o'clock, an advanced hour for the call to be anything but an emergency. Oscar and Elinor were sitting on their upstairs porch as usual and Oscar went to answer it. He came back in a few moments and said, a little uneasily, "It's Florida Benquith, she sounds worried."

Elinor got up and went to the telephone. Oscar hung about and listened to his wife's end of the conversation. This wasn't much, for Florida was a great talker and on this occasion she had more than usual to say.

"Listen, Elinor," she began without preamble, "I'm sorry to call you like this, but I thought you ought to know what happened—or what we *think* has happened, because we're not sure yet. I've just now sent Leo on over there."

"Are you talking about Queenie?" asked Elinor calmly.

"Of course I am! I was standing in my kitchen, Elinor, putting away plates. My window's open for a little breath of air and suddenly I hear all kinds of carrying-on coming from Queenie's house—and it's not Queenie going on after those two children either, it's Queenie's voice and a man's voice and who is Queenie arguing with? is all I can think. So I turn out the light and step out on the back porch so they cain't see me—I didn't want 'em to think I was spying, and anyway I wasn't, I just wanted to make sure Queenie was all right—and I'm listening but I cain't tell what anybody is saying but they keep

136

on with it. Then I hear Queenie holler 'No!' and then I don't hear anything else. Elinor, I tell you, I was starting to get worried."

"What'd you do?" said Elinor.

"I run to get Leo. He's in the living room, reading. I bring him out on the porch and I tell him what I heard and we just stand there listening, but we cain't hear much. We cain't hear anything at all, in fact, and I tell him what I heard before and he says, 'It's probably James Caskey over there telling Queenie she's spending too much money down at Berta's, that's probably what you heard.' I say to him, 'If it's James Caskey visiting over there, then why are all the lights out?' And he doesn't know. So we just stand there in the dark, and then I say to Leo, 'Leo, maybe I ought to give a call over there and make sure she's all right.' And Leo says, 'That's a good idea,' and I'm just about to go inside and pick up the telephone when Leo whispers to me, 'Stop.' So I stop and I look out across the yard and there is somebody coming out of the back door of Queenie's house and it's a man."

"What man?" asked Elinor.

"That's just it, we have no idea what man. But, Elinor, both Leo and I were almost positive *it was a levee-man*. He snuck around the front of the house and looked around and then he took off like lightning. I *know* it was a levee-man, I just know it and I think something happened to Queenie, so I sent Leo right over there. I told him don't even knock, just go on in, and he did it. So he's over there now and I'm on my way over and, Elinor, I think you better come too."

Florida hung up and Elinor turned to her husband and said: "Well, Oscar, it looks like one of your levee-men has gone and raped Queenie Strickland."

In the darkened room Queenie sat weeping on the edge of the bed. She had pulled on a skirt, but hadn't

137

bothered to button it. Her underslip was soiled and torn, and she had drawn a house jacket around her bruised shoulders. Florida had made some of Elinor's special Russian tea and taken it to her, but the cup sat untasted on the small table beside the bed. Elinor and Oscar arrived, and Florida said immediately, "Well, Elinor, you've just got to talk to her. She won't *let* us call Mr. Wiggins." Aubrey Wiggins was the chief of the three-man Perdido police force.

Leo Benquith came in from the kitchen.

"Is she all right, Dr. Benquith?" Elinor asked.

Dr. Benquith shook his head. "Elinor, what happened here tonight..."

"I know, I know," said Elinor soothingly as she sat down on the bed and put her arm about Queenie's shoulder.

Oscar, standing ineffectually by, could only think to say, "Queenie, did you have your door locked?"

Queenie paid no attention to anyone, but continued to sob convulsively.

"Where are the children?" asked Oscar.

"They slept through everything, thank the Lord," said Florida. "So I sent them over to my house. They're fine."

"You didn't tell those children what happened, did you?" asked Elinor sharply.

"'Course not!" replied Florida. "But, Elinor, we got to do something. That levee-man walked into this house, and he"—out of consideration for Queenie she did not finish the sentence; but then she went on quite as if she had—"and so we *got* to call up Mr. Wiggins."

Queenie reached over and squeezed Elinor's hand pathetically, as much as to say, *Don't*...

"No," said Elinor. "Don't call Mr. Wiggins. We don't want to say anything. And, Florida," Elinor went on, turning to Florida and eyeing her with purpose, "you are not to say *anything* to *anybody*, you hear?"

"Elinor—" began Oscar, but was interrupted by Leo Benquith.

"This could happen to other people, Elinor. We got to find the man who did this and string him up on the nearest tree. Or buy him a ticket on the Hummingbird—or something. Queenie, you think you could recognize the man who came in here tonight?"

Queenie drew in her breath sharply and held it. With weary eyes she looked around the room and held each person's gaze for a moment. She swallowed back another sob and then said in a low voice, "Yes. I know the man who did it."

"Well, then," said Leo Benquith, "we ought to get Wiggins over to that dormitory right now and drag that man down to the jail. Soon as you feel—"

"No!" cried Queenie.

There was a moment's silence, then Elinor asked, "Who was it, Queenie?"

Queenie sat very still and tried to control her shaking. She closed her eyes and then said, "It was Carl. That's who it was. It was my husband."

Nothing was to be done, then. Leo and Florida Benquith went home; there wasn't any danger that the doctor would say anything, for doctors, after all, held many confidences. Both he and Elinor extracted ironbound oaths from Florida that she would say nothing to anyone. Leaving Malcolm and Lucille with the Benquiths, Elinor and Oscar took Queenie home with them. They went very quietly into the house, hoping to escape the eagle notice of Mary-Love next door.

Upstairs in the bathroom Elinor stripped off Queenie's clothes and set her in a bathtub filled with hot water and sweet-smelling salts. Queenie sat unmoving as Elinor washed her all over. That night

Queenie and Elinor slept together in the large bed in the front room.

The next morning, as Queenie picked at her breakfast, Elinor sat by the window and cut up all the clothing that Queenie had worn the night before. She made Queenie watch as she tossed the scraps into Roxie's stove.

Somehow, Carl Strickland had found Queenie out. Probably it hadn't been difficult, for the Snyders—Queenie's family—were nearly all dead, and the ones that weren't dead were dirt poor. It could only have been logical to look for Queenie in Perdido, where her rich brother-in-law owned a sawmill and forest land that a million birds could nest in. Penniless, indigent, forsaken by what little respectability his wife had afforded him, Carl bummed his way down from Nashville. He had been casually offered employment on the levee. He took it, worked part of one day, and found out the whereabouts of his wife that very evening. He cajoled his way into her house and demanded money and support. Fighting with her when she refused him, he hit her, ravished her, and slipped away into the darkness.

Early next morning, Oscar drove down to a work site near the town hall where he knew the most inexperienced men had been set to work and without any difficulty found Carl sullenly helping to turn over a wagonload of clay. Carl was tall and thin, with a coarse face that showed in every crease the man's ill-humor toward the world. Oscar casually called him over and said, "You're Carl Strickland. I believe I met you at Genevieve's funeral."

The easy tone of his voice made Carl grin, for he knew all of Queenie's in-laws were rich, and he somehow had it in his mind that they would just as soon assist him as not. "That's right. I 'member you, too. You're Mr. Caskey, you're old James's nephew, right? Genevieve sure had it easy, living with a man like that. You got as much money as him?"

Oscar smiled, looked around curiously at the work progressing about them, glanced down at his shoes, then up at Carl again, and said, "Mr. Strickland, I got a little something to say to you..."

"What?"

"You better pack your portmanteau and hop on the back of the next conveyance out of this town."

Carl's grin and his expectations winked out quite as suddenly as they had winked on. He said nothing, but there was an unpleasant expression in his eyes.

"Mr. Strickland," Oscar continued after an unflinching moment, "I believe you paid a visit to your wife last night."

"I did," said Carl shortly.

"Queenie complained to me of that visit. I think Queenie would be pleased if you didn't knock on her door anymore. I think it would suit us all pretty well if you gave up this job—it's mighty hard work, Mr. Strickland, and that sun is awful hot"—Oscar squinted up into the morning sky—"gave up this job, Mr. Strickland, and went someplace that was cool...and pretty far away."

"I cain't afford to," said Carl Strickland. "I cain't afford to go nowhere. Besides, Queenie is my wife. I got a right to be in this town. I got a right to hold down this job. You cain't just come out here and say—"

"Mr. Strickland, you have been relieved of your position on this levee. There is *nothing* to keep you here in Perdido." Oscar took an envelope from his pocket. "Now, considering your long service with our town in the construction of the levee and the great benefits that have accrued from your labor, Mr. Strickland, the town of Perdido is very proud to present you with seventy-five dollars in U.S. currency." He stuck the envelope in the pocket of Carl's shirt.

"Also inside you will find a schedule of the trains that are going north from Atmore station and the trains that are going south. The town wasn't certain in which direction you would be traveling this afternoon, Mr. Strickland."

"I ain't going nowhere."

Oscar turned and glanced at the automobile in which he had arrived. As if this were a signal of some sort, a second man, who had been sitting inside fanning himself with the brim of his hat, stepped out of the automobile and wandered over to where Oscar and Carl were standing.

"Sure is early in the day to be so damn hot," said the man, nodding to Carl as he spoke.

"Mr. Wiggins," said Oscar, "this is Carl Strickland. He is distantly related to us Caskeys by marriage."

"How-de-do?" said Aubrey Wiggins, a thin man who sweated and suffered in the sun as much as if he had weighed twice as much as he did.

Carl returned the nod.

"Mr. Wiggins is the head of our police force," explained Oscar. "Mr. Wiggins is gone drive you up to Atmore."

Aubrey Wiggins withdrew a yellow kerchief from his back pocket and wiped his brow. "Mr. Strickland, don't you start worrying, I'm gone make sure I get you there in plenty of time. Which way you gone be going now? Are you going toward Montgomery? Or will you gone be traveling through Mobile? Oscar, my mama was born in Mobile, you know that?"

"I met your mama once," replied Oscar. "She was real sweet to me."

"I love that woman," said Aubrey Wiggins, a faraway look momentarily clouding his eye. "Mr. Strickland, you want a ride over to the dormitory? I s'pose you got a few things you want to pack."

"I ain't going nowhere," said Carl.

142

Oscar looked at Carl, then at Aubrey Wiggins. Then pulling his watch from his pocket, he said, "Good Lord, look at what time it is! Aubrey, I got to be moving along or that mill is gone fall apart without me. Nice seeing you again, Mr. Strickland. You be sure and send me a postcard with a picture of some ice on it, you hear?"

"I ain't going nowhere!" Carl shouted after Oscar's retreating figure. Oscar smiled, got into his car, and waved as he drove off.

Aubrey Wiggins, who had put up his soaking kerchief, got it out again, and wiped his neck. "Mobile train is at two, Montgomery train is at three. We could make either one of 'em. You got any preference, Mr. Strickland?"

CHAPTER 24

Queenie and James

Everyone in Perdido found out what happened to Queenie Strickland, even though all those involved in the incident professed to have remained silent. Florida Benquith was suspected of retailing the incident, but she never admitted to her indiscretion. Fortunately for Queenie's peace of mind, the matter was laid to rest after a few days' intense gossip by Queenie's unwillingness to speak of the unhappy experience at all or even to acknowledge to herself that it had happened. Three or four months later, however, interest in the matter was renewed, for Queenie Strickland's propensity to roundness of figure increased noticeably.

It was no use for Queenie to deny her pregnancy, or the fact that the impregnation had been highly unwelcome. It was all as generally known as though it had been printed on the front page of the Perdido *Standard* with a photograph of Queenie, her two children at her side, captioned: "Expectation of a Third."

Mary-Love was mortified. This was a blow to the Caskey name, for Queenie was, in everybody's eyes, under the family's protection. That a woman related to her in any way should bear a child by the involuntary coupling with a levee-man—even if she *had* been married to him—was a disgrace to the family. Mary-Love couldn't be brought to speak to Queenie, and declared that the woman ought to be strapped to her bed for the duration of the pregnancy; Mary-Love shuddered every time she heard that Queenie had been seen on the streets. "That woman is carrying her shame—and our shame—before her!"

James Caskey was brought down by the news as well. He imagined—rightly—that Mary-Love would construe the misfortune as his fault: for having in the first place married Genevieve Snyder, which brought Queenie to town, who attracted that villain Carl, who...and so forth. This unfortunate business in Queenie's present made James wonder about Queenie's past. During the seven years of James's marriage to Genevieve Snyder, Genevieve had spent a total of at least five of those years in Nashville with her sister. James had of course met Queenie on several occasions, and had once visited her home in Nashville for the purpose of securing Genevieve's signature on some important papers. He had known that Queenie was married to a man called Carl Strickland; James had met him once and thought him a sullen, unimproved sort of fellow, but respectably dressed and not an obviously vicious type. Here now was that same man, employed as a levee-worker, wearing ragged ill-fitting clothing, and raping his wife. James was very sorry for Queenie, but he could not help wondering how Genevieve could have spent five years in the same house with this terrible man. Genevieve hadn't been a pleasant sort of woman, it was true, but she had always been well bred. In this respect she was the superior of Queenie, and it was hardly conceivable to James that his wife would have consented to share a home with a brother-in-law who could so easily sink to the level of a migrant worker. There was something wrong with the picture James had always had of Genevieve living quietly and decorously with her sister and her brother-in-law in their white frame house in Nashville. If he had been wrong on this point, then might he not have been mistaken on others as well? It was this sudden uncertainty concerning his wife's past that sent James over to Elinor's one afternoon in November to ask her what she knew of Queenie and Carl's life together in Nashville.

"I don't know anything about it," replied Elinor.

"Queenie loves you," said James. "If she would tell anybody then she would tell you."

"She hasn't told anybody then. I don't know why you need to know anyway, James." Elinor was a bit curt. "Queenie has had enough trouble, and her trouble isn't over yet."

"Is that man coming back?!"

"No, no," said Elinor quickly. "Oscar would shoot him. Or Queenie would. Or I would. But she's going to give birth to that man's child."

"Well, the child is legitimate at least."

"He *raped* her. That won't be a happy child, James. Now, why do you want to know about Queenie and Carl?"

Oscar explained why he was uneasy; Elinor seemed mollified. "All right, I see. I really *don't* know anything about their life together. Why don't you go ask Queenie herself? She'll tell you, just explain everything to her."

James reluctantly admitted that he could probably satisfy himself in no other way, though he dreaded to intrude upon his sister-in-law. After her trouble had been revealed to him, James had gone around to all the stores in town and lifted the limits he had placed on Queenie's spending. He had not talked to her, and suspected that, since she hadn't taken advantage of this largess, she knew nothing of his little gesture of sympathy.

Now, from Elinor's house, he telephoned Queenie, and said in the cheerful coo that his voice always assumed over the telephone: "Hey, Queenie, it's James. Listen, I'm over at Elinor's and she told me you weren't doing anything tonight. You think you could come over to my house and sit for a spell? It's been so long! No, you bring Lucille and Malcolm over to Elinor's and they can play quiet with Zaddie. I'm gone send Grace over here too so you and I can talk by ourselves!"

When he had hung up, he said apologetically, "Elinor, I have just managed to fill up your whole house with children for the entire evening."

"It's all right, James. They may be rambunctious everywhere else, but those children always play quiet here. I don't know why that is."

"They won't disturb Frances?"

Elinor laughed. "Don't you worry. I can't *get* them up here on the second floor. They say they're afraid of this house. They say there's ghosts and things in the closet, even though this is practically the newest house in town."

James looked about him a little uncomfortably, and thanking Elinor again, took his leave.

James hadn't laid eyes on Queenie recently, and the greatest difference in her seemed not her enlarged belly, but her dazed calmness. It was as if she had been severely chastened, and for what transgression she had no idea at all. At the same time James looked at her through Mary-Love's eyes. James had a tendency to do this, for Mary-Love represented to him the chief arbiter on matters of morality. In that perspective, Queenie appeared somehow more respectable. They sat together in James's formal parlor, James in a rocking chair, Queenie in the corner of Elvennia Caskey's blue sofa. Queenie at first wouldn't look directly at James, but ceaselessly rubbed the nap of the velvet upholstery first one way and then the other, giving that action total attention with her eyes.

"James," she said, "I feel so guilty for not coming over here and thanking you as soon as I found out."

"Found out what, Queenie? Sure is good to see you again," he added parenthetically.

"Good to see you, too. Found out about my little bills around town. Berta Hamilton showed me everything she had in the place and said I could take away anything I wanted. Everywhere else too. James, down at Mr. Gully's, I was offered a fleet of automobiles that would have put down the Kaiser."

"Queenie, if you want to put down the Kaiser, I'll buy you those automobiles!"

Queenie laughed, but the laugh faded quickly enough. "James Caskey," she said, looking up at him and for the first time catching his eye, "I thought I was gone be happy the day I showed up in Perdido. I thought I was gone be happy for the rest of my life."

"Nobody's happy for the rest of their lives, Queenie."

She shook her head. "I guess not. James Caskey, what'd you want to say to me? Why'd you call me up out of the blue?"

"I wanted to ask you something."

"Ask me what?"

James's mouth twitched, and he paused. "Ask you about Carl, I guess."

"I thought everybody knew."

"Knew what?"

"This is Carl Strickland's baby." She patted her belly.

"Of course it's Carl's baby," James assured her. "Carl is your husband. Whose else baby would it be? Queenie, I want to know about you and Carl in Nashville. That's why I asked you to come over here."

"What about us?"

James shrugged; he didn't know how to put politely what he wanted to ask.

"James," said Queenie after a moment, "Carl Strickland wasn't around much."

"Ah!"

"Is that what you wanted to know? Carl Strickland drinks, Carl Strickland does a lot of things, Carl Strickland doesn't have very nice habits, and— praise be to God—he was away most of the time. How you think Lucille and Malcolm would have turned out if I had let their Daddy pick 'em up and talk to 'em all the time? Oh, I know what those children are like, I know they're not ever gone be welcome in this house till they can walk through a room and not pick something up and smash it on the floor, but I have done the best I could..."

"Queenie—"

"Ohhh!" cried Queenie in an exhalation of breath which produced something between a squeal and a sigh, "Genevieve couldn't *stand* him! She couldn't stand to be around him!—and he couldn't stand her. When she'd come up there and see me, he'd go away. So when I couldn't stand to be around Carl Strickland one minute more I'd call up Genevieve and say, 'Genevieve Snyder, you come up here tomorrow morning.' James, I 'pologize for that, I 'pologize for keeping your wife away from you—'cause that's just what I did."

Queenie didn't exactly look as if she were about to cry, but she began smoothing and ruffling up the nap of the upholstery once again.

"It's all right, Queenie. I'm glad you told me." It made him think better of his dead wife, that she had abandoned him and his daughter for reasons that were partially unselfish. His uncertainties, too, were now resolved, but what was left was a little curiosity, so he asked, "Queenie, when Carl would go away, where would he go?"

"I don't know," answered Queenie. "I never asked. But he couldn't have gone far, because the minute Genevieve walked out the door with her suitcase he was back. Maybe he was living in the house across the street, and just watching us out the window. He was sneaky like that."

"What'd he do for work?"

"He worked for the power company. He cleared land." Queenie stopped fidgeting with the nap of the sofa and looked up again into James's eyes. "James, you have been good to me. And here I am sitting on this sofa, just lying to you. I'm not exactly lying, I guess, I'm just making things sound better than they really were. Carl Strickland is no good. He was no good the day I married him, he was no good the day he showed up in this town, and he was no good every day in between. He *did* do work for the power company—or at least he used to, but he got fired when they found out he was stealing things. I don't even know what kind of things. And he was in jail—twice. One time for beating up a man about something and one time for cutting a woman's arm with a razor-knife. See, that's when Genevieve came to stay with me, when Carl was in jail, 'cause I was afraid to be alone and 'cause I didn't have any money and that's how Malcolm and Lucille and me lived, on that money you sent Genevieve every month. And when Carl would get out of jail, then Genevieve would come back here to stay with you.

"James, Genevieve wasn't an easy woman to get along with, I know that, but you didn't know our daddy either. James, our daddy beat Genevieve. One day he fired a gun at her, and if I hadn't thrown a platter at his hand the bullet would have gone right through her head. Daddy got killed out in the woods—I don't even know how, and I don't think I want to know—and Genevieve and I were all by ourselves. Pony was already off in Oklahoma. We took care of ourselves; Genevieve went to school and I went to work, and when Genevieve needed help I helped her and when I needed help she helped me. Neither of us would ever have won any prizes for anything, but she was good to me and I was good to her. It was like cutting off my arm when I opened that telegram and found out she was dead. James Caskey, you have been so good to me—when you didn't have to be—that I thought you should know all this. Nobody else knows it, not even Elinor. I guess I would appreciate it if you would not spread it around."

James was silent for several moments, though obviously greatly perturbed. Finally, he rose and paced up and down behind the sofa on which Queenie still sat, now again smoothing and ruffling up the nap of the blue upholstery. "Queenie, isn't there *something* I could do for you? Isn't there something you want I can buy for you? You know, don't you, that I'm always gone take care of you, and I'm always gone take care of Lucille and Malcolm?"

"Long as they don't come in here and break things, you mean?" said Queenie, with a little giggle that was reminiscent of her old way, before the trouble had come upon her. "James Caskey, there's nothing I want. Or wait, there is one thing, just one thing..."

"What is it?"

Queenie stood up and straightened her dress. She turned and faced James and she looked at him seriously. "Sometime I want you to send me a telegram. And the boy will come up to the door, and say, 'Miz

152

Strickland, here's a telegram for you,' and I'm gone give that boy a silver dollar, and I'm gone sit down on the front porch and open that telegram, and it's gone say, *Dear Queenie, I have just put Carl Strickland twenty feet under the ground in a marble casket with combination locks.* That's the one thing you can do for me. You can send me that telegram."

CHAPTER 25

Laying the Cornerstone

Interesting as were Queenie's problems, the subject couldn't hold up for long against the all-consuming fascination with the levee. The project had continued apace, and with far fewer snags than appeared in the brief lengths of the Perdido and Blackwater rivers as they flowed through the town limits. The bond issues had been approved by the legislature, the bonds sold and the money gathered in and deposited in the Perdido bank. Already the levee had been completed on both sides of the river south of the junction, and the townspeople congratulated themselves on the fact that were the water to rise tomorrow, only the two sawmills and the stately homes of the Caskeys and the Turks and the De-Bordenaves would be destroyed. All the rest—the town hall, downtown, the workers' houses, Baptist

Bottom, the homes of the shopkeepers and professional people, and even the dormitories and kitchen of the levee-men themselves would be only as wet as falling rain could render them. Just before Christmas of 1923, the first wagonloads of dirt were poured out at the edge of the junction, and the second levee began to creep northeastward along the Blackwater River toward the cypress swamp, to render safe the Caskey, Turk, and DeBordenave mills, whose prosperity had made the building of the levees possible in the first place.

The levees may have been no more than massive lengths of packed red clay, but already Perdido was growing so accustomed to their presence that they began to seem not so unattractive after all. The roses, the dogwoods, the holly, the smilax—and above all the kudzu—had taken root, and there was more green and less red to be seen every day, at least on the townsides. The narrow path atop the levee on the western side of the Perdido had become a favorite promenade for the white population after church, and mistresses waved to their maids disporting themselves on the far side of the river in *their* best clothes. People would look at the levees and exclaim vehemently, "Lord, I am just about to forget that the levee is there, I am getting so used to it!" Or people would remark, "It was always so *flat* around here, I don't know why we didn't think of this before!" Or they judged, "The levee is gone be worth every penny we pay for it, just to know that our children aren't ever gone have to learn what it's like to go through a flood."

Soon the levee along the Blackwater was completed. A hundred yards beyond the Turk mill it ended in a steep ramp that descended onto the low mound of an Indian burial place. This ramp became a favorite spot for the boys of Perdido—led in mischief by Malcolm Strickland—who rode their bicycles on top of the levee all the way from the workers' dormitory, past Baptist Bottom, turning at the junction as the levee turned, past the sawmills, and out into the piney forest again. The rivers were at the left and the town below to their right. The boys wondered if they could ever get nearer the sky, and were certain that the Rocky Mountains themselves could be no higher than their town's levees. At the end, they let go of their bikes' handlebars, threw their arms up into the air, and sailed down the ramp across the top of the Indian burial mound. They then grasped their handlebars again and applied their brakes at the last possible moment before coming to grief in the thicket of briars and broken bottles and other detritus of construction work that lay on the other side of the mound.

The levee along the Blackwater had been finished in very good time, and now there remained only the levee along the upper Perdido, which would protect no more than the millowners' houses. Early Haskew and Morris Avant had worked wonders with the construction so far, and were actually under budget.

Work continued without interruption, beginning at the thicket between the Turk house and the town hall. The levee-men went at it with a will, for the end of the project seemed in sight. But, oddly, progress here began to slow down. Early Haskew wasn't sure why. Perhaps it was an instability of the bank along this section of the Perdido, but every night half the clay that had been brought to the riverside during the day slid down into the water and washed away with nothing to show for the effort but a slightly redder tinge to the already red Perdido water. The other portions of the levee had seemed almost to build themselves, the work had gone so easily—or so it seemed now in comparison with this final recalcitrance. No headway could be made. Tons and tons of clay and gravel and plain old dirt were brought in every day and piled up and packed tight, but half of what was built up was certain to be eroded away in the night.

Early was frustrated, and Morris Avant cursed a great deal. The levee-men became restless and anxious, acting as if there were something perhaps more supernatural than geological at work in the matter. Many of the men declared that they had heard about a lake being dredged over in Valdosta, and that the pay for unskilled workers was higher, so they left Perdido with what little money they had managed to put aside. Some of them actually did go to Valdosta, but others appeared to have wanted only to put Perdido behind them. The black men employed on the levee were suddenly overwhelmed by the necessity of putting new roofs on their Baptist Bottom homes. Others developed bad backs, or lost temporarily the use of their right or left arms. So while the work to be done had doubled in difficulty, Early's work force decreased by half. Sometimes it looked as if the levee behind the millowners' mansions never *would* be finished.

"I don't know," said Oscar to his wife one evening, as he stood on the screened porch staring out at the still distant limits of the levee construction, "if they are *ever* gone get up this far."

"They won't," said Elinor, matter-of-factly.

"What do you mean?"

"The river won't let them finish," explained Elinor, but for Oscar, that was no explanation at all.

"I still don't understand what you're trying to say, Elinor."

"I'm trying to say that the Perdido isn't going to allow the levee to be finished."

Oscar was perplexed. "Why not?" he asked, as if the question were sensible.

"Oscar, you know how I love that river—"

"I do!"

"Well, this town *belonged* to that river, and the levees are taking it away, and the Perdido isn't getting anything in return."

"You think everybody should stand on the edge of the water and throw in hard cash or something?"

"You know," she said, "at Huntingdon I took classes about the ancient civilizations, and what they used to do whenever they built something real big—like a temple or an aqueduct or a senate house or something—they would sacrifice somebody and bury him in the corner of it. They'd tear off his arms and his legs while he was still alive and pile all the pieces together and then cover it up with stones or bricks or whatever they were building with. The blood made the mortar hold together, everybody thought. And it was their way of dedicating it to the gods."

"Well," said Oscar, a little uncomfortably, "James is gone arrange the dedication ceremony when the levee finally *does* get finished, but I don't think he is planning anything along *those* lines. Is there maybe some *other* way to pay the river back that you can think of?"

Elinor shrugged. "I certainly have been wracking my brain trying to think of one."

A few days later, Queenie Strickland gave birth to a boy. The baby would not have lived had Roxie—in attendance with Elinor and Mary-Love—not unwrapped the umbilical cord from around the child's neck, where it was choking him. The night that her son was born, Queenie Strickland woke sweating from a nightmare in which her husband Carl was walking up and down on the front porch, seeking a way into the house. She swept her sleeping infant up into her arms and held him tightly against her breast, hoping to still the harsh beating there. Oscar had placed a loaded shotgun in the corner of the room, and the sheriff had promised to hang her husband on sight if he ever came to town again, but Queenie knew that one night she would hear those booted footsteps on the front porch in cold reality.

That same night, at the precise moment that Queenie Strickland woke from her nightmare and clutched her newborn child to her, John Robert DeBordenave awakened also. The unlighted room and the night outside were no darker perhaps than the inside of John Robert's mind; in fact, he scarcely knew that there was any difference to be drawn between the states of waking and sleep. Poor John Robert was now thirteen, and was to be advanced this coming autumn into the fourth grade, as little prepared for that promotion as to be instantly declared Under Secretary of the Interior in charge of water projects. Grace Caskey and numberless other children had left him behind, and the farther John Robert was left behind, the gloomier he became. It was no longer enough to be tickled in the ribs once a day as his pockets were rifled for candy; not enough to watch his classmates' mysterious games from the corner of the building where he rubbed his back ceaselessly against the rough bricks as an exercise in sensation. His sister Elizabeth Ann ignored him now, and seemed embarrassed by his presence. His mother and father smiled at him and hugged him and shook him lovingly by the shoulders. All this was no longer enough for John Robert, and though he knew he wanted something more from life, he had no idea what that something more might be.

More candy. This thought now came from some dark corner of John Robert's half-mind.

More candy was not the answer, but John Robert's stunted brain couldn't conceive of anything better than that.

A ray of light from the setting moon was suddenly cast onto the floor of John Robert's room. He got up out of the bed and stood near that spot of light; he stuck his foot into it, knelt down and stuck his hand into it. Then, in that position, he gazed up and out the window at the moon itself. The moon was waning and gibbous, but John Robert had no more idea of the moon's periodic alteration of shape than the moon had of John Robert's vague desires for more candy. He went to the window and looked out over the lawn at the back of the house. The levee, despite all the problems, had been inexorably extended, and now the major part of the work had been done across the back of the DeBordenaves' property, and was just now beginning at the Caskeys', so directly before him and to the right rose its black bulk. Here and there a band of paint around the handle of a spade or perhaps the metal of the spade itself left by the workers glinted in the moonlight. And to the left of the construction he dimly saw the Perdido, with a single line of the moon's reflection quivering on its black surface. James Caskey's house, glowing a cool bluish-white in the moonlight, stood stolid and square in the plot of sand that began where the DeBordenaves' grass left off abruptly. And there in that sandy yard were the oak trees that John Robert loved so much—two in particular, that he could see if he leaned out a little farther. These were about four feet apart, and grew straight up to the sky. Between these two trees, some years before, Bray Sugarwhite had nailed a board to form a little bench, and John Robert had watched with wonder as the bark of the oak trees had grown around the ends of the boards, surrounding them and holding the board fast, as if the trees had laughed at Bray's nails and had said to each other, *Hey, we're gone show Bray how to do this thing right.* Sitting on that board day after day, coming inside only for meals, John Robert had watched the progress of the levee as it crept slowly toward him along the bank of the river.

John Robert now leaned out the window, and saw, sitting on his favorite bench, Miss Elinor. She was wearing a dress that glowed the same bluish-white as James Caskey's house. She smiled and waved to him, and held her finger to her lips for silence.

Not knowing why, and never considering that perhaps he ought not, John Robert pushed a chair against the wall beneath his window, climbed onto it, unlatched the screen, wriggled out, and dropped into his mother's bearded-iris bed beneath, scraping himself against the side of the house in the process. The sharp leaves of the plants ripped his pajamas in two or three places, and underneath sliced his skin, but John Robert was so accustomed to small injuries that he scarcely noticed them. He picked himself up and ran barefoot through the dewy grass to the edge of his lawn.

Miss Elinor still sat upon the bench, though now she leaned against one of the trees and patted the seat beside her in invitation to John Robert to join her.

John Robert hesitated, then with no more concrete reason for going on than there had been for the hesitation, he lifted his foot from the dewy grass and placed it down on the raked sand.

The sand stuck to the soles of his feet as he made his way across the yard. He timidly seated himself by Miss Elinor and looked up into her face. He could no longer make out her expression, however, for the shadow of the tree trunk shaded it into blackness.

John Robert said nothing, but he hummed a blurred little tune and waved his short little legs beneath the wooden plank, kicking up sand. He felt Miss Elinor's arms comfortingly encircling his shoulders. He stared before him at the dark hulk of the levee, and continued to hum.

The boy perceived nothing strange in Miss Elinor's sitting on the bench at such an hour, in her beckoning him, in her silence, or in the tender grip with which she now embraced him. John Robert DeBordenave took notice and affection however and whenever it came, and never questioned its source or motive. He was content to sit and hum and kick his legs in and out of the shadows of the trees, so that now and then a spray of sand fell twinkling like a shower of minuscule stars. And when Miss Elinor rose from the seat beside him and with no apparent effort lifted him up and set him on his feet and pushed him in the direction of the levee, he did not resist her gentle urging for a moment. She walked behind him with her hands on his arms and directed him toward the most advanced point of the levee construction.

The levee-men on this day had upturned their carts of red clay, for the first time, onto Caskey land. Clods of clay had spilled out over Zaddie's rake designs and shone black now on top of the gray sand that gleamed in the moonlight. Tomorrow the men would begin in earnest, and within a week or so the river would no longer be visible from the windows of James Caskey's house. The generous grounds behind the houses would be narrower by twenty-five feet or so.

John Robert was not allowed this close to the river, and obedience being such a habit with him he was uneasy despite the presence of Miss Elinor behind him.

When John Robert stopped, instinctively knowing that he ought to go no farther, Miss Elinor's grip on his arms became suddenly tight and painful. He could no longer move either his arms or his body, so tight was Miss Elinor's hold. He twisted his head around and looked up at her in meek protest.

But it wasn't Miss Elinor's face that returned his gaze. He couldn't see much of it because the moon was hidden directly behind that head, but John Robert could see that it was very flat and very wide and that two large bulbous eyes, glimmering and greenish, protruded from it. It stank of rank water and rotted vegetation and Perdido mud. The hands on John Robert's arms were no longer Miss Elinor's hands. They were much larger, and hadn't fingers or skin at all, but were no more than flat curving surfaces of rubbery webbing.

John Robert turned his face slowly and sadly back to the river. He stared before him at the levee construction and the muddy water that flowed silent and black behind it. What little mind and consciousness the child possessed was being burned away by Miss Elinor's betrayal, by her becoming something else, by her transformation into this terrible thing that held him in its grip. He began to weep, and his tears flowed softly down his cheeks.

Behind him he heard a little hiss of wetness, as when the belly of a large and still-living fish is slit open with a knife. One of John Robert's arms was raised out from his body, and he continued to weep.

There was a wrench and a tear, and a jab of pain so violent and strong that John Robert couldn't even identify it as pain. Then the child saw—but did not know what he saw—his own arm tumbling through the moonlight. It landed with a thump on the red clay at the very edge of the Caskey property. The moon shone down upon it, and ten feet away John Robert DeBordenave saw the fingers of his own disembodied hand grasp and squeeze the clods of clay that lay beneath it.

His other arm was raised and wrenched out of its socket. It, too, sailed through the air and landed across the other; this time the palm lay upward so that the clawing fingers clutched nothing but air.

John Robert now felt his body engulfed with warm liquid, and did not know that it was blood. Coherent thought had never come easily to John Robert, and now it had entirely forsaken him. He slumped to the ground, and one of those webby appendages that were not hands at all was pressed against his chest. With a splintering of bone, a stripping of tendon, and a tearing of flesh, first one leg and then the other was twisted all the way around in its socket. John Robert saw them arch through the air and fall twitching on top of his detached, crossed arms.

The last thing that John Robert DeBordenave perceived was the slight whistle of wind in his ears and a light breath of wind across his face as all that was left of him, his trunk and head, were picked up and hurled through the air. He turned and twisted, and saw his own blood streaming from the holes in his body, gleaming in thousands of black droplets in the moonlight. He jerked once when he fell atop the pile of his own limbs, and was conscious for one second more as he saw a sheet of clay and gravel from the top of the levee come sliding down on top of him. A small stone struck his right eye, bursting it open like a spoon plunged into the yolk of an egg. John Robert DeBordenave, his twisting head at last stilled beneath the small avalanche of pebbles and clay, knew no more.

CHAPTER 26

~~~~~~

The Dedication

Caroline DeBordenave was frantic for days after her son's disappearance. The noise of the levee-men, which had never bothered her before, seemed to drive directly through her skull now, and she demanded that her husband halt all the work until their boy had been returned to them.

No one had any idea where to *begin* to look for John Robert. The unlatched screen told how he had got out of the house. His missing pajamas told what he had been wearing, but of his disappearance no one could say more. Teenaged boys bearing stout sticks for defense against rattlesnakes walked through the woods and called his name. People in Baptist Bottom looked under broken-down wagons to see if the white boy had taken shelter there. The mayor of Perdido made a tour of inspection of the marble-floored room beneath the town hall clocks, but John Robert wasn't among the bats and bird-nests up there. Zaddie wriggled around in the crawl spaces beneath the millowners' mansions, but found nothing but rodent nests and spider webs.

After ten days, Caroline DeBordenave had to accept what everyone else in Perdido had known from the beginning: John Robert had drowned in the Perdido. Children in town didn't get bitten by mad dogs or fall down empty well shafts or suffer fatal accidents while playing at "barbershop" or discharge loaded pistols into their throats. In Perdido, unlucky children drowned in the river, and that was that. Except for the junction, the young members of Perdido's population led a charmed life. But the river took its sacrifice frequently, and sometimes the bodies were recovered by a fisherman far downstream. Most of the time, even when the dying throes of the girl or boy were witnessed by a dozen little friends, the body was never found. The child was dragged down to the bed of the river and buried there beneath a coverlet of red mud, to sleep undisturbed until the Resurrection should rouse those tiny bare bones to partake in Glory.

The search for John Robert went on longer than any had before. The boy's dim intelligence *might* have led him someplace other than the Perdido, and Caroline DeBordenave cried out that her son would no more go near that river, having been warned against it all his life, that he would have driven a heated spike through his own hand. The DeBordenaves, too, were millowners, and their son, feeble in mind and body though he might be, was a personage of importance. And his feebleness made John Robert an object of greater pity than if he had been a ruffian white boy whose father was a drunk, or some untraceable black girl who was only number three of her parents' eight children and had shown not the least aptitude for cooking or laundry.

Despite the intensity of the search and despite Caroline's complaining, work on the levee did not halt. In fact, it hastened. Whatever it was that had held back work on the upper Perdido stopped on the day of John Robert's disappearance. Thereafter, the curtain of earth flew up, rod by rod, and before the Caskeys knew it, the view of the river from each of the three houses was blotted out. Even when Oscar stood on tiptoe on the sleeping porch he couldn't peer over the top of the levee to see the water on the other side. He could scarcely see the tops of the live oaks on the far bank of the Perdido.

Oscar had dreaded this moment, for he knew with what baleful foreboding Elinor had spoken of the time when the river should be obscured from their windows. Elinor surprised him; she hadn't complained, even of the noise and the litter of the workmen. In fact, she sent Zaddie and Roxie out with pitchers of iced tea and lemonade at noon. She hadn't been out of sorts at all. When she wasn't visiting with Queenie and her new little baby, Elinor sat on the porch and rocked in the swing and read magazines and only made little grimaces when occasionally some workman's blasphemy or obscenity sounded clear upon the breeze.

One Sunday afternoon when Oscar and Elinor were together on the upstairs porch, Oscar stood up, went over to the screen, and with a broad gesture pointed far to his left. "They gone take the levee about a hundred yards beyond the town line, just to make sure everything's all right. You never know, the town might grow in that direction and somebody'll want to build out there. But the way they going now, they gone be finished in another two or three weeks." He paused, turned, and looked at his wife, wondering if he had perhaps gone too far. But Elinor continued to rock with perfect placidity. Oscar ventured to remark, "You know, I really used to have the idea that you were gone be upset when the workmen got up this way."

"I thought I was, too," replied Elinor. "But it doesn't do any good to get upset, does it? I couldn't stop the levee all by myself, could I? And didn't you say that you would never get any money from the bank unless the levee was built?"

"That's right. We're all set now," replied Oscar.

Elinor said, with a small embarrassed smile, "I guess I feel a little better about that old levee now."

"What made you change your mind?" Oscar asked curiously.

"I don't know. I guess I thought Early and Mr. Avant were going to cut down all my water oaks, but Early told Zaddie this morning that he would be able to leave every one of my trees standing."

"I don't suppose, though, I'll be able to persuade you to go to the dedication ceremony?"

"Oh, Lord, no!" Elinor laughed gaily. "Oscar, I've already had a little party for the levee."

The levee was finished, and the levee-men were paid off. They dispersed with such rapidity that the five colored women who worked in the kitchens were left with four hundred pounds of beef, and three hundred pounds of pork, and one thousand pounds of potatoes. Eventually, through the largess of the town council, that surplus found its way into the skillets and pots of Baptist Bottom. The dormitories in which the levee-men had lived for nearly two years were swept out, boarded over, and locked tight until some use could be found for the buildings. The

170

last bits of work on the curtains of clay that now protected every square foot of built-up Perdido could easily be accomplished by the twenty black men who remained in Early Haskew's employ.

The two white women who lived in Baptist Bottom returned to Pensacola when their red-light custom evaporated. Lummie Purifoy's gambling hall closed, and his daughter Ruel took up candy-making. The Indians out on Little Turkey Creek closed down two of their five stills. And Perdido, in general, breathed a little easier.

The dedication ceremony, arranged by James Caskey, was held in the field behind the town hall; a triangular podium had been built in the corner where the upper Perdido levee met the lower Perdido levee. James Caskey made the introductory speech, and the town of Perdido cheered him and the levee. Morris Avant rose and promised that he would sit down at a table and eat the Methodist Church steeple if one drop of riverwater ever appeared on the town side of the levee. Early Haskew got up and claimed that there wasn't a finer town or friendlier people to be found in all of Alabama, and just to prove it he had gone and married Sister Caskey and they were already happier than pigs in sunshine. Tom DeBordenave and Henry Turk and Oscar Caskey then each in turn stood and proclaimed an era of unmitigated prosperity for Perdido on account of the levee. As the audience bowed its head, and the preachers prayed their prayers of dedication to the God of the Methodists and the Baptists and the Presbyterians, the downspout in the center of the junction, directly behind the speaker's stand, but invisible to all because of the curtain of clay, swirled the red water of the Perdido and the blacker water of the Blackwater faster than ever, dragging down to the bed of the rivers more detritus, living and inanimate, than it usually did, as if it wished it might draw in the whole town of Perdido—industry and houses and inhabitants and all. But the combined power of those two rivers and the desperate strength of the maelstrom at their junction had no effect on the levees, and the waters flowed and plunged and swirled and eddied and glided on, seen only by those brave and mischievous children who played atop the levees and by those who glanced curiously down into the water from the safety of the bridge spanning the river below the Osceola Hotel.

Perdido was no longer the same town, so much of Elinor Caskey's prediction had proved true. Perdido no longer *saw* the rivers that had given the town much of its character, except when it promenaded along the levee or crossed from downtown over into Baptist Bottom. Now Perdido saw the levee, the newer parts of it still red, but the first-built parts now covered over with the dusty deep green of the kudzu vine.

During those speeches on the day of dedication, Perdido looked around at what had been built, and now, quite suddenly Perdido seemed to see the levee with strange eyes: it looked as if some unimaginably vast snake had slithered out of the pine forest and curled itself around the town, and now lay sleeping, an unwitting protector of those whose habitation was within its shadow.

Perdido looked around at the levee that lay coiled on every side, and at the end of James Caskey's ceremony, the applause perhaps wasn't as enthusiastic as it had been at the beginning.

One warm evening in September of 1924, about a week after the dedication of the levee, Tom De-Bordenave knocked on the door of Oscar Caskey's house. Zaddie let him in and showed him up to the

172

screened porch on the second floor where Oscar and Elinor sat in the swing. Tom admired the baby in Elinor's arms; he admired the house he had walked through; he admired the view of the levee from the second floor of Oscar's house. Probably he would have gone on forever in admiration of something or other had not Elinor discreetly taken her leave and left him alone with Oscar.

"Oscar," Tom began, breaking off in the middle of an encomium upon the generous dimensions of the sleeping porch the moment it seemed Elinor was out of earshot, "we are in trouble." Not yet knowing whom "we" was intended to signify, Oscar said nothing. "The flood hurt us—real bad."

"It hurt everybody," agreed Oscar with cautious sympathy.

"It hurt us worst of all. I lost my records, I lost my inventory. If it could float, then it got washed away. If it could spoil, then it rotted away to nothing. If it could sink, then it sank, and I never saw it again."

"Tom, you've recovered," said Oscar kindly, confident that by "we," Tom referred only to the De-Bordenave mill. "You've got everything going again. Of course it takes time—"

"It takes money, Oscar. Money I haven't got."

"Well, now that the levee's built, you can borrow it from the Pensacola banks. Or the Mobile banks."

"Oscar, cain't you understand? I don't *want* to straighten things out. I want to get out of the business." He sighed. "I want to get out of Perdido."

Quietly, Oscar said, "Are you talking about John Robert?"

"Caroline won't even pick up the telephone when it rings. She thinks it's gone be some old fisherman saying he has caught John Robert on his hook and could we please come and pick him up. And I'm about as bad as she is. Poor old John Robert, I just know he drowned in the Perdido, but, Lord God! I wish we could find his poor old body so we could know for sure. It sure would be a comfort to put him in a decent grave. Oscar, Caroline is about to go out of her mind. Elizabeth Ann is away at school and I'm at the mill, and she's alone in that house all day. I just don't know *what* we're gone do. Except I do know we're gone get out of Perdido. Caroline has people up near Raleigh, and we're going there. Her brother has a tobacco concern, and I'm sure he'll find me something to do. We sure are gone miss this place, but, Lord God! we got to get away and stop thinking about poor old John Robert. So that's why I'm here, on account of John Robert. I came to see if you wanted to buy the mill."

Oscar whistled for a few moments, leaned forward and put his hands on his knees. Then he said, "Tom, listen, I'm not the man you should be coming to. You know that James and Mama are the only ones around here with money."

"I know that. I also know that you make the decisions. You know, Oscar, you may think Henry and I don't know what's going on, but I tell you we do. We know what's going on because Caroline and Manda have told us what is going on."

Oscar's brow was furrowed. "Elinor has been saying something?"

"Not much," said Tom. "But enough so that Caroline and Manda figured it out. Elinor thinks you don't have enough on your own. And Henry and I think that, too. That's why I am offering *you* the mill and that's why I am *not* offering it to James and Mary-Love."

The two men remained another couple of hours on the darkened porch. Their business, the most momentous deal that had ever been considered in the history of the town of Perdido, might have been about the price of a load of kindling, their voices were so soft and conversational. Real business in Alabama wasn't conducted in offices or in mill-yards or across store counters. It went on on porches, in swings, in the moonlight, or perhaps in the corner of the barbershop on the shoe-shining perches or in the grassy plot behind the Methodist Church between Sunday school and morning service or in the quarter-hour that preceded Oscar's Wednesday night domino game.

" 'Course," said Tom DeBordenave, "the real question is, have you got the money?"

"Mama and James do. Or they could get it. I haven't got a penny except my salary and a little bit of stock."

"Borrow it from the bank. James will cosign even if Mary-Love won't. And I tell you what, you pay me half tomorrow, you can pay the rest over five years, ten years, that doesn't matter much. I'd like to be rid of it and I'd like it to go to you."

"Tom, something worries me."

"What?"

"Henry Turk worries me. Henry's not gone be happy if I suddenly buy you out and he's left sitting there in the Caskey shadow."

"Henry's in a little trouble, too," said Tom. "You know that. Henry couldn't afford to buy me out. There'd be no point in my even speaking to him."

"I don't like making Henry feel bad," said Oscar, shaking his head.

"I don't either, but what can I do? I want to sell my place."

"Sell Henry part of it," Oscar suggested.

"What part?"

"Anything he wants—your customers, your inventory, your notes outstanding, your equipment, your mill-yard—whatever he wants except the land. I want all your land. You make sure I get every acre."

"You're asking me to go to more trouble."

"You'll get more money out of it if you sell to two instead of one. And I want old Henry to feel good about this. If he buys up your mill over there it'll *look* to him like he beat me out, and he'll feel fine. All Henry wants is a bigger yard to walk around in, and all I really want is the land."

"Oscar, let me tell you something. I think you're foolish buying up all this land. You don't even cut what you've got now. You haven't got the mill capacity to do it."

"Oh, Tom, you're right, you came to the right man when you wanted to sell, 'cause I know I'm no good at this sort of thing. But the fact is, Mama and James and I decided that we wanted land, so whenever we see it coming down the road we flag it down and hop on."

The men talked at greater length, though to no altered purpose. In the way of Southern business, any agreement of this complexity must be talked over until every point has been argued out and agreed upon at least three times, by way of fixing it not only in the minds of the parties involved, but in their hearts as well. At Elinor's direction, Zaddie brought up a tray with two small glasses and a bottle of pre-Prohibition whiskey on it, and the third reiteration of the agreement was worked through rather more quickly with the help of the liquor.

The next morning, Oscar led James Caskey out into a remote corner of the pine forest and told him of Tom's offer. James thought it an excellent opportunity for Oscar, and by Oscar's decision to take only the land, the whole thing might be kept more or less a secret from Mary-Love. She would otherwise object to any plan by which her son achieved any semblance of financial independence, even if that semblance

176

were no more than a debt for a quarter of a million dollars.

Within the week, a kind of treaty had been worked out among the three millowners for the division of the DeBordenave holdings. Henry Turk, as Oscar had predicted, took over the physical plant along the Blackwater River—all the land there, the buildings, the inventory, and the machinery. This cost him three hundred thousand dollars, which he was to pay in eight installments without interest. This excellent bargain Tom DeBordenave was able to accede to because Oscar was paying him an equal amount, in cash borrowed from the Pensacola bank, for the thirty-seven thousand acres of timber he owned in Baldwin, Escambia, and Monroe counties.

Two lawyers came down from Montgomery, put up at the Osceola Hotel, and worked for a week straight on the business of deeds and transfers. Only when everything had been signed was the announcement made of the partition of the DeBordenave property. This was a vast shock in Perdido, and all the townspeople walked about in a daze, wondering how the change would affect them personally.

Tom and Caroline, bereft of their son, their property, and their position, quickly packed and left for North Carolina. Mary-Love and Manda Turk had time to do no more than take Caroline to lunch one day in Mobile and present her tearfully with a diamond-and-ruby brooch in the shape of a peacock. At this meal Mary-Love learned that it was Oscar, not herself and James, who possessed the former DeBordenave acreage. She was so humiliated and angered by James and Oscar's high-handedness in the matter that the next day without a word to anybody she took Sister and Miriam and Early on a two-week's trip to Cincinnati and Washington, D.C.

"They'll be back," said Elinor, without concern.

"Mary-Love and Sister will take good care of Miriam. I'm not worried."

Nothing, in fact, could have disrupted Elinor's equanimity at this time. The big money of Perdido, which formerly had been partitioned equally among three families, was now divided between only two. Oscar, who had had no share of the wealth before, was now a man rich in timber-bearing land spread over three counties. Although Elinor might no longer be able to see the river from where she rocked in the swing, she continued to spend her afternoons on the upstairs porch, where she bounced Frances up and down on her knee and cooed, "Oh, my precious baby! One day your daddy is going to own *all* the mills along the river. And one day we are going to have a whole *shoebox* full of land deeds, and every acre of land we own will have a river or a creek or a branch or a run on it for my precious baby to play in. And Frances and her mama will have more dresses and more pearls and more pretty things than everybody in the rest of Perdido put together!"

John Robert DeBordenave lay immolated in the levee, the town's right and savory sacrifice to the river whose name it bore. John Robert's death had permitted the levee to be completed and had given Oscar Caskey ownership of the land that would make the Caskey fortune even greater than Elinor herself dreamed. John Robert's parents had gone away from Perdido and gravel had stopped his mouth from calling out to them. Red clay had prevented his detached arms from waving them to return. Black dirt had held down his severed legs from running after them. But, torn, pinned, and buried though he lay, John Robert DeBordenave wasn't finished with Perdido, or the Caskeys, or the woman responsible for his death.

178

CHAPTER 27

The Closet

In the years following, Perdido grew considerably. The levee had been the primary cause for this increase in population, wealth, and prominence. Not all the men who had worked on it went away when it was finished. Some were offered jobs at the mills, took them, and settled down. The banks in Pensacola and Mobile, seeing that the future of the mills was protected by the embankments of earth, were now willing to lend money to the millowners for the expansion of their businesses. Both the Caskey and the Turk mills took advantage of this, bought more land, ordered more equipment, and together helped to finance a spur of railroad track from the mills up to the L&N line in Atmore. With this useful track and the larger trucks being produced by Detroit, the rivers were employed less and less for the transportation of felled trees and lumber. No longer were the Perdido and Blackwater rivers of overwhelming economic importance to the town.

Except for the business of the mutually advantageous construction of the railroad spur, the two lumber mills drew apart. Henry Turk's only idea was to do what he had always done, only much more of it. Oscar and James Caskey, on the other hand, realized that demand for lumber might not always be what it was today, and so decided to diversify. Accordingly, in 1927, James and Oscar purchased the dormitories on the other side of Baptist Bottom, and converted the buildings to a sash-door and window plant. Perdido's unemployment plummeted to nothing at all. The following year, a small veneer plant was added next to it, thus making it possible to utilize the bottomland hardwoods that did not otherwise provide profitable cutting.

Henry Turk laughed up his sleeve at the Caskeys, for these operations were patently not as profitable as the mere production of building lumber. The Caskeys were in debt for the capital they had needed to start up their new business, they had vastly larger payrolls, the demand for window sashes and hardwood veneers was troublesomely erratic and likely to remain so. The Caskeys ignored Henry Turk's laughter, and waited only for these new operations to become solvent before they established a plant to produce fence posts and utility poles.

It was Oscar's intention to appoint within the Caskey dominion a use for every part of a tree. Nothing should go to waste; everything should be turned to productiveness and value. Early Haskew was redesigning the town's steam plant so that it would run on the bark and dust that were a by-product of the cutting operations. Already the burning of waste was heating the kilns that dried the lumber and the pulp.

180

Of equal importance to Oscar was the maintenance of the forests. He hired men from the Auburn forestry department to come down and talk to him. Under their guidance, he instituted a system of selective cutting and intensive replanting. It was Oscar's goal—quickly achieved—to plant more trees than he cut down. He set up an experimental station near the ruins of Fort Mims, in hope of creating a more vigorous strain of yellow pine. He corresponded with agriculture departments all over the South, and at least once a year made inspection trips to other lumberyards from Texas to North Carolina.

Oscar's energy was surprising. He had certainly never done so much before. It was his work that had kept the mill going so well for the past decade, but all this extra business was something new. Perdido wasn't used to such quick expansion, such explosive innovation. Perdido tended to agree with Henry Turk, and considered that Oscar was spreading the mill and its resources too thin. Mary-Love occasionally complained to James that her son was running the mill into the ground, but James refused to interfere. Mary-Love wouldn't speak to her son directly about the family business because she knew that he would not heed her advice. She didn't want to put herself in the position of having any request refused.

As the years passed, it became gradually known that Elinor Caskey was actually the force behind her husband's spirited plans. If she didn't actually make the suggestions herself, then she at least kept him firmly spurred in those general paths of diversification and innovation. It was Elinor who sent him off to Spartanburg, South Carolina, to look at the big mills there, and over to Little Rock to see the new wire-box factory. Why Elinor would cause her husband to expend so much energy in a concern by which he would personally gain so little was unknown. If the mill made a great deal of money, then all the profit would be divided between Oscar's mother and uncle. He still would get only his salary. Mary-Love was a hearty, strong woman, not likely to die soon, and at that, no one put it past her to leave all of her money to Sister and Early Haskew, in order to spite Elinor even from the grave.

Oscar was still very much in debt from the purchase of the DeBordenave land in 1924. He received money from the mill for trees harvested on his land, and this was used to pay the interest on the loan, but very little of the principal had yet been repaid, and what was left over from the lumber receipts kept his wife and daughter in decent clothes, but didn't pay for much else. He and Elinor were still very much in straitened circumstances.

"I sure do wish I could afford to take you to New York for a week or two," Oscar said to Elinor with a grimace.

"Don't even think about it, Oscar!" Elinor replied with unfeigned indifference. "You know we can't afford it, and besides, the Perdido River doesn't flow through New York, so why on earth would I want to go *there?*"

So long as she seemed assured of her husband's working hard and attempting to turn everything to advantage, Elinor was content. Mary-Love was always traveling to Mobile and Montgomery and New Orleans, buying dresses and lace tablecloths, when Elinor scarcely had an extra dime to replace the brown thread she had run out of. But Elinor did not complain. She sat in her house all day on the upstairs porch, rocking and sewing. She taught Frances, now five years old, to read and to write, so that she wouldn't have any difficulty when she began school. On most days, Elinor climbed up to the top of the levee, grasping the trunks of water oak saplings she had planted in its clayey sides, and strolled along the top, gazing in absorption into the red swirling water of the Perdido.

Frances could not remember a time when the sandy yard in back of the house led directly down to the river. She had known only the levee there, that thick sloping bank of red earth and clay, slowly covering itself in a mantle of water oak and kudzu. She wasn't allowed to climb it, unless her mother carried her up, and she wasn't allowed to stick her hand beneath the broad flat leaves of the rampaging kudzu, for snakes bred there in profusion. "And other things, too," Ivey Sapp claimed, "things just waiting to bite off a little white girl's hand." Frances was jealous of the children who were allowed to play on the levee, like Malcolm Strickland, who was constantly riding his bike back and forth its entire length whenever he wasn't in school. Elinor took her daughter boating in Bray Sugarwhite's little green boat. Frances couldn't hear often enough about how her mother had been rescued out of the Osceola Hotel by Oscar and Bray and taken to safety in this very same boat with Bray plying these very same paddles. Frances was frightened whenever they approached the junction and always held on tight to the sides of the boat. She tried her best not to show her fear, for that was disrespectful of her mother, who Frances thought was capable of just about anything. Elinor was certainly capable of shooting past the junction without Bray's little green boat being sucked down to the bottom of the riverbed, and proved it to Frances many times.

There was something otherworldly about floating down the river between those manmade hills of red clay. Frances knew that the houses and shops and sidewalks of Perdido lay just on the other side, but gliding along, she wasn't able even to see the clock tower of the town hall, and got no sense of human life being so close. She and her mother were in a solemn wilderness as deep and sublime as if they had been a thousand miles away from anyone but each other. "Oh," Elinor sighed once, and Frances didn't know whether her mother spoke to her or mused only to herself, "I used to hate the levee, hate the very idea of it, but days like this I row down the river and I remember what it was like before there *was* a Perdido and sawmills and bridges and cars."

"You *remember*, Mama?"

Elinor laughed, and seemed drawn back. "No, darling, I just imagine it..."

The town intruded upon the peace of the river between the levees only at the bridge that crossed the Perdido below the Osceola Hotel. Cars passed over the bridge now and then, and children on their bicycles, and there was almost always an old black woman, with a cane fishing pole and a cage of chirping crickets for bait, leaning on her elbows on the cement railing trying to save her husband the price of a slab of pork for supper.

Frances would have enjoyed these excursions except for a vague feeling she had that her mother expected her to say something or *feel* something that she neither said nor felt. Gazing into that swift-flowing water that was so muddy one couldn't even see a foot beneath the surface, Frances would have to shake her head no when her mother would say, "Don't you want to just dive right in?" Frances had learned to swim at Lake Pinchona, had taken readily to the clear artesian well water that filled the pool there, could dive and swim beneath the water and hold her breath longer than any of her friends. Her mother promised that if Frances ever wanted to swim in the Perdido she would protect her from the whirlpool at the junction, from the leeches along the banks, from the water moccasins, and from whatever else hid itself in the muddy current. "But you wouldn't even have to worry about those things," Elinor assured her daughter, "because you're my little girl. This river is like home to me. One of these days it'll be like home to you, too."

Elinor never pressured Frances to swim in the river, and Frances never told her mother that it wasn't fear that kept her from making the attempt, but rather the unsettling familiarity she felt with the Perdido. Not understanding that familiarity, she didn't want to pursue it. Frances may have been only five, but was already possessed of vague memories of a time that seemed impossibly earlier. The Perdido belonged to that time, as did a child—a little boy her cousin Grace's age—whom she sometimes remembered having played with in the linen passage between the front room and her own. But so far as she knew, she had never swum in the Perdido, and the little boy ranged in her memory without a name.

Frances was a tender child, and not much given to complaining. She never compared her lot to others', never said to another little girl, "I hate doing this, don't you?" or "It makes me so mad when Mama says that to me." She imagined that every emotion that overtook her was peculiar to herself, could never be shared with anyone else, and certainly was never experienced by anyone else in Perdido. Thinking her own feelings of very little consequence, Frances never spoke them aloud, never sought to be praised or reassured or disabused or confirmed in anything she thought or felt.

Foremost among these rigidly maintained silences were Frances's thoughts concerning the house she lived in. She knew a little of its story: her grandmother had built it as a wedding gift for her mother and her father, but had refused to let them have possession of it for a long while. Then Miriam had been born, and Mary-Love had said, "Give me Miriam and you can move into the house." That was why Miriam lived with her grandmother, and that was why Frances was all alone.

In this story Frances saw nothing unusual, nothing cruel, nothing unfair. What concerned Frances was not the story of the bartering of Miriam for her parents' freedom, but rather what had happened in the house itself during the time that it lay empty. This concern was prompted by Ivey Sapp, Mary-Love's cook, who had told Frances the story in the first place one day while Frances was sitting in the kitchen of her grandmother's house.

Frances had been entranced by the idea of sheets placed over all the furniture.

"You mean," Frances had asked, "that my house just sat there all locked up and empty? That's funny."

"No, it ain't," returned Ivey. "Not funny one bit. Ain't no house that's empty. Something always moving in. You just got to make sure it's *people* that gets in there first."

"What you talking about, Ivey?"

"Nothing," replied Ivey. "What I'm saying is, child, is you cain't have a big house like that just sitting there with nobody in it, and all the furniture covered up in sheets and them little stickers still on the windowpanes and all the keys in the doors, and not have somebody move in it. And when I say *somebody* I don't necessary mean white folks and I don't necessary mean black folks."

"Indians?"

"Not Indians neither."

"Then what?"

Ivey paused, then said: "If you ain't seen 'em, then it don't matter, do it, child?"

"I haven't seen anybody there but Mama and Daddy and Zaddie and me. Who else lives there?"

They were interrupted by Frances's grandmother, who came in just then and remarked, "Does your mama let you gallivant all day long without supervision, child?"

Frances was sent home before she could discover who else might inhabit the house in which she lived.

Frances recalled that conversation for a long time, though she forgot completely why she had been in Mary-Love's kitchen when she was so rarely at her grandmother's house and almost never there alone. Sometimes she even thought it had been only a dream, it seemed so disconnected from any other memory. But she never could figure out whether Ivey's pronouncements affected her attitude toward her home or whether it only confirmed something she had already begun to feel.

Frances thought she ought to love the house. It was big—the biggest in town—and had many rooms. She had a room of her own and her own bath and her own closet. The hallways were wide and long. There was stained glass in all the outside doors and on the parlor windows, so that in the afternoon the sun painted all the floors in brilliant colors. If Frances sat in that colored light and held a mirror out in front of her, she herself was painted vermilion and cobalt and sea green. The house had more porches than any house in town. On the first floor there was an open porch in front, narrow and long, with green wicker rocking chairs and ferns. Above it was another porch, opening from the second-floor hallway, the same size, with more rocking chairs and a table with magazines. In back on the first floor was the kitchen porch, latticed over so that it remained cool in summer. On the second floor in the back was the biggest of all, the sleeping porch, screened, looking out at the levee and Miss Mary-Love's house, with swings and hammocks, ferns, hooked rugs, gliders, fringed standing lamps, and little tables. Frances's own bedroom had one window that looked out over her grandmother's house, and one that opened directly onto this screened porch. It was the most delicious feeling, Frances thought, to go to the window of her room and look out and see what was essentially another room. At night, when she went to sleep, she could turn in her bed and look out that window through soft gauze curtains and see the silhouettes of her mother and father, rocking slowly in the swing and speaking in soft voices so as not to disturb her. Sometimes Frances stood on the sleeping porch and looked through the window into her own room and was always astounded at how different it appeared from that perspective.

Outside, the house was painted a bright white, as were nearly all the houses in Perdido, but the interior was dim and dusky. The sunlight never penetrated far into the rooms. The paper on the walls was all in dark subtle patterns. On all the windows were amber canvas shades, venetian blinds, gauze curtains, and then lined draperies. In the summer, all these were kept tightly drawn against the heat, and opened only at dusk. Moonlit nights frequently brought more natural light into the house than the brightest summer afternoons.

The house also had an odor that was peculiar to it, a mixture of the sun-bleached sand that surrounded the house, of the red clay of the levee, of the Perdido that flowed on the other side of the levee, of the mustiness of the dark walls and wide dark rooms, of Zaddie's cooking in the kitchen, and of something that had come with the emptiness of the house and never quite gone away. Even in months of drought, when the farmers' crops shriveled in the fields and the forests were so dry that a stroke of heat lightning could ignite whole acres within five minutes, the house had a slight odor of river water, so that the papered walls seemed damp to the touch and new envelopes stuck down and pie pastry didn't come out right. It could seem that the entire house was enveloped in an invisible mist that had risen from the Perdido.

These were Frances's principal perceptions of the house in which she lived, but there were impressions that were more obscure, less tangible, felt immediately upon waking and immediately lost, or fashioned in the last moment before sleep and never recalled, or sensed so fleetingly as never to be recovered whole. But a hundred of these impressions, added up and tied together with the string of Ivey's words and hints, left Frances with the distinct impression that she and her parents and Zaddie were not alone in the house.

Frances's fear of the house was confined to the front room—the bedroom at the front of the second floor. One window of this room overlooked her grandmother's house, and a second opened onto the narrow front porch. The room had been set aside for guests, but Frances's parents never had visitors who remained overnight. Between this room and Frances's was a small passage with a door on either side fitted with cedar shelving for the storing of linens. It seemed to Frances that whatever was in the front room could come right through that passage and open the door of hers without her parents—across the wide corridor—knowing anything of it. Every night before Frances would get into bed, she'd make certain that the door of that passage was locked.

When Zaddie was cleaning the front room, Frances sometimes ventured in, despite her ravening fear. She'd hang about and in great dread search for evidence to confirm her fear that the room was inhabited. Even as she did this, Frances knew in her heart of hearts that whatever lived there lived not in the room proper, but in the closet of that room.

In the center of the back wall of the front room was a fireplace with black and cream tiles and a coal-burning grate. To the left of this was the door to the passage that led to Frances's room and to the right of it was a small closet. Here were agglomerated Frances's first fears of the house. The door of that closet was the most frightening thing Frances could imagine existing anywhere. It was misshapen, smaller than any other door in the house, only about four and a half feet high, when all the others were at least seven. To Frances's emotional reasoning, it seemed that anything that hid in that closet must be smaller than anything that might wait for her beyond any other door, and she feared dreadfully that aberration of size. In this closet, Frances's mother kept the clothes she wore least, but still wanted to preserve: out-of-season dresses, overcoats, shoes, handbags, oversized hats. It smelled of naphtha, feathers, and fur. Opened, the closet presented one flat expanse of leather and cloth and dark spangles. Because there was no light in it, Frances had no idea how far it extended either to the sides or to the back. To her imagination, it had no firm dimensions at all, but expanded or contracted according to the whim of whatever creature took its shelter within.

Any house built on pilings, as all the Caskey houses were, is bound to shake a little under stray footfalls and other movements. Glass rattled in the dining room cabinets. Doors slipped on their latches. This Frances understood logically, but it still seemed to her that that closet was the echo point for all the vibrations in the house. That closet shook with every step that was taken. It treasured up stray noises. When it thought no one was paying attention, it instituted the noises and the vibrations and the shakings itself.

All this Frances knew, and of all this Frances would say nothing to anyone.

However, when it appeared that she was to be left

alone in the house, as sometimes happened in the afternoon, Frances made some excuse to visit Grace two houses down, or begged permission to walk over to the Stricklands. If permission was denied, or no excuse could be found to go away, Frances did not remain alone inside. She waited patiently on the front steps until someone returned. If it was raining, she sat on the front porch in the chair nearest the steps, so that if she heard something moving inside, she would have a clear exit out into the yard. At these unhappy times, Frances did not even turn and peer through the stained glass into the parlor windows, fearful of what might peer back at her. To the little girl the house seemed a gigantic head, and she only a morsel of meat conveniently positioned in its gaping mouth. The front porch was that grinning mouth, the white porch railing its lower teeth, the ornamental wooden frieze above its upper teeth, the painted wicker chair on which she perched its green wagging tongue. Frances sat and rocked and wondered when the jaws would clamp shut.

As soon as anyone returned, the house seemed for a time to lose all its threatening malevolence. Frances skipped blithely in behind Zaddie or behind her mother, and wondered at her own foolishness. In that first flush of bravery, Frances would run upstairs, fly to the door of the front room, peer in, and grin at the fact that there was nothing there at all. Sometimes she'd pull open a drawer of the dresser, and other times she'd drop to her knees and check under the bed—but she'd never go so far as to touch the knob of the closet door.

END OF PART II

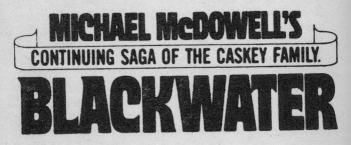